To the Moon and Back

SECOND EDITION

Advance Praise for To the Moon and Back

To the Moon and Back is a wonderful story of life, family, love, faith, dementia, and caregiving. As I travel a similar path with my mother, I could relate to the characters. Their struggles and successes are very real and can be embraced by anyone caregiving for someone with dementia. More correctly put, for the "Care-partners" on the journey of dementia. This book introduced me to that phrase, and I love it! If you are a Care Partner who is looking for a good story you can relate to, *To the Moon and Back* is the perfect choice. I will be recommending it to my clients.
—**Carol Howell**, Amazon #1 Best Selling Author, *Let's Talk Dementia*, Executive Director, Senior Life Journeys, www.seniorlifejourneys.com

Compassionate, compelling, and complex—in one amazing story. Kathi Macias writes a touching story that connects faith, family, and the difficult issues of Alzheimer's disease, disabilities, and what really matters most. She addresses a plethora of family dynamics—a prodigal child, a depressed and disabled husband, and a gentle soul whose forgetfulness becomes a heart-wrenching diagnosis. What a blessing it was to peek into the heart and mind of one stricken with Alzheimer's so I can better understand those I love who struggle with similar issues.
—**Susan G Mathis**, author *The Fabric of Hope: An Irish Family Legacy* and others.

In *To the Moon and Back*, Kathi Macias has taken her readers on a very touching journey with a family whose husband and daughter must come to terms with their beloved wife and mother who has Alzheimer's. They must depend on support and encouragement from other people. Each day brings new challenges, as different emotions surface. You will marvel as you watch God work in their lives, showing His grace and mercy.

—**Marcia Hyland**, pastor's wife, Bible study instructor, and mother of an adult son with a TBI, Jamars5722@verizon.net

In *To the Moon and Back*, Kathi Macias presents a story that might be familiar to many but is framed in a new, dynamic fashion. It is a novel that speaks to the fragility of relationships, while centering on one of today's hot-button issues. In these pages, Alzheimer's steals memories, while also paving the way for a deeper understanding of the power of hope, love, and faith. *To the Moon and Back* is a realistic modern drama, anchored in grace as old as time itself.

—**Ace Collins**, author, In the President's Service series, Christy Award winner, *The Color of Justice*.

To The Moon and Back begins with a cloud of confusion, leading to a diagnosis of Alzheimer's. Kathi Macias skillfully lifts the fog of bewilderment and masterfully guides the reader to an unexpected outcome of faith, inspiration, and hope. You will want to share this book with anyone dealing with the issue of Alzheimer's, for in it is found remarkable insight, encouragement, and reassurance.

—**Marilyn Orton**, president, Women of Worth International, www.wowintl.net.

I'm not much of a nonfiction reader, so when I can find the same type of emotionally charged topic in a fiction work, I'm sold. *To the Moon and Back* deals with a family that must find a way to survive a past tragedy, only to be thrown into the evil grasp of Alzheimer's. When played out on pages of fiction, this topic is able to touch all of us in a mighty way. We don't think, *Oh, that family went through it, so I won't have to.* Because true stories always happen to the other guy, right? But we know how fiction touches all of us, and Kathi Macias did just that in *To the Moon and Back*. There is no escaping life's struggles, and her characters deliver the answers with grace and courage. If you read romance, you need to read this novel. What a love story! And not only the love of a man and wife, but of a family, and their relationship with God. If you read one book that will change your life this year, read *To the Moon and Back* by Kathi Macias.

—**Linda S. Glaz**, author of *Fear Is Louder than Words*

Kathi Macias is well-known for her ability to pull us into a compelling story. I'm telling you now, there's no shortage of "compelling" in this one! *To the Moon and Back* is real and lovely and heart-wrenching, and all the while overflowing with grace and hope. It's the kind of hope that offers encouragement and strengthens faith. I love the reminder that our God is at work in every circumstance. The book poignantly connects with the issues of illness/disability, caregiving, dementia, and more, and those issues are approached with insight and courage. It's exactly that approach that makes me ever gladder I have this book!

—**Rhonda Rhea**, TV personality, humor columnist, author of twelve books, including *Turtles in the Road*, www.rhondarhea.com.

To the Moon and Back

SECOND EDITION

Kathi Macias

Copyright Notice

Cover and Interior Design: Derinda Babcock
Editor(s): Linda Wood Rondeau, Deb Haggerty
Author Represented By: Hartline Literary Agency

PUBLISHED BY: Elk Lake Publishing, Inc., 35 Dogwood Drive, Plymouth, MA 02360, 2021

_____

Library Cataloging Data
Names: Macias, Kathi (Kathi Macias)
To the Moon and Back / Kathi Macias
236 p. 23cm × 15cm (9in × 6 in.)
ISBN-13: 978-1-64949-375-0 (paperback) | 978-1-64949-376-7 (trade paperback) | 978-1-64949-377-4 (e-book)
Key Words: Alzheimer's Disease, dementia, family, relationships, loss of cognition, aging, romance
Library of Congress Control Number: 2021945901 Fiction

Dedication

To all whose minds and memories are affected by Alzheimer's, and to the ones who love and care for them ... take heart! God stands ready to carry you all the way.

Prologue

The moon was a pale sliver that mid-October night in the small coastal town of Wildflower, Oregon. The diminutive but still attractive sixty-seven-year-old shivered as she stood in the shadows near the rose bushes that had stopped blooming weeks earlier. She clutched her sweater a little tighter across her middle.

Were evenings always so chilly here? For some reason, she couldn't quite remember, but it didn't really matter. Somewhere, in the nostalgic canyons of her mind, she recalled another moon—a harvest moon. And she remembered a voice promising he would always love her "to the moon and back."

She smiled, wondering if the man who spoke those words so very long ago ever thought of her now. Did he still love her "to the moon and back"? Had another love taken her place? Or had he already stepped into eternity?

Her smile faded at the thought. She had no idea if the man, whom she considered her first and only true love, had ever made his peace with God. She was certain he hadn't at the time he declared his love for her—didn't even believe in God, or so he claimed. She had been a Christian since her childhood, and she imagined that was the reason the two of them had eventually gone their separate ways. The thought saddened her, as it always did.

"Rachel!" The voice called her back from a precipice of darkness, one looming closer and threatening her more often. She pushed the fear away and tried to focus on the present.

"Rachel!" The voice was more impatient this time. "Where are you? I need you to help me with something."

She sighed, as thoughts of a harvest moon and a promise from another time faded from her consciousness. Pete needed her, as he always did. His need for her brought comfort but also frightened her. She slipped away more often these days and could no longer be trusted to do what she must. Not a good thing—for her or for Pete.

"I'm coming," she called, leaving the cool shadows of the backyard—so many parties and get-togethers held there over the years. Would there ever be another celebration in this place? Unlikely. The thought scarcely registered as it skittered through Rachel's mind.

Chapter 1

Each time Rachel found herself wondering when and how it all started, she quickly became frustrated because she often forgot what *it* was. Today was no different, and so she dismissed the thought and went on to the next thing.

Like Mama taught me. "*When you feel confused or at loose ends, baby girl, just lean on God and do the next thing.*"

Rachel smiled. She might be getting old and a bit forgetful, but memories of Mama and Daddy were as clear as ever—clearer, maybe, since she seemed to reflect on them more often these days. She so delighted at being able to hear their voices once again, offering correction or encouragement when most needed.

She'd been blessed to grow up in a loving, God-fearing family where, if anything, she was spoiled because she was an only child.

And yet her parents had taught her to be kind and humble and grateful, so how spoiled could she really be? She shook her head at the thought and reverted back to the idea of doing the next thing.

"Now, what *is* the next thing?" Rachel frowned as she scanned the nearly immaculate kitchen. "Looks like I've already done the dishes, so that's not it." She passed through the kitchen and stopped in the laundry room, where a handful of dirty clothes sat atop the washer. "That must be it. The next thing is doing the laundry."

She started the water running and tossed in the detergent, then checked the pockets of a pair of her husband's slacks. *Why didn't he ever learn to check his own pockets? You'd think he could remove a few coins and a soiled hanky, instead of leaving it for me to do."*

She reminded herself of his restricted mobility since the accident, and her heart softened. She hummed, "I'll Fly Away" as she lowered the lid and flipped off the laundry room light.

"Now, on to the next thing." She returned to the kitchen. Still clean. Pleased she wasn't letting the dirty dishes get ahead of her, she wandered out of the kitchen and down the hallway toward the bedrooms. She was relatively certain the sheets in her room were clean, and in her daughter's room as well, since Lilly was away at college. What about the guest bedroom? She couldn't remember the last time she'd changed the bed in there. Today might be the perfect day, especially since she was already doing laundry.

She opened the door and entered the room, smiling as she always did at all the familiar reminders of her childhood. So many of the unique items her parents had left to her were prominently displayed in what she had long referred to as her "retro-room." The dark mahogany bedframe, the hurricane lamp on the dresser, the frilly white curtains and lace doilies, and her mother's rocker—at least it was her mother's until she went into the rest home. A twinge of sadness pinched Rachel's heart, and she sat on the edge of the double bed. Rubbing her hand across the quilted blue and white spread, the pain turned bittersweet as she remembered this same quilt being on her own bed when she was a child.

"I miss you, Mama and Daddy," she whispered. "I—"

"So this is where you are. I've been looking everywhere for you."

The accusatory words interrupted her thoughts, dispelling the melancholy feelings that had brought tears to her eyes. Quickly brushing them away, she put on a smile and looked up. Pete stood in the doorway, wearing his faded pajamas and scruffy slippers, leaning on his walker and frowning. He seemed to frown a lot these days, and Rachel didn't think his scowls helped his frumpy appearance.

Now what? Something's always bothering him. But then again, it's not his fault. If it hadn't been for the accident …

He interrupted her again, his slightly rheumy gray eyes mirroring the irritation in his voice. "I'm hungry, Rachel. You said you were going to make lunch an hour ago. What have you been doing?"

She opened her mouth to answer but couldn't find the words to defend herself. Ah, well, what did it matter? Pete was seldom pleased with anything she did for him, though the good Lord knew she tried.

Rachel rose from the bed, still wearing her smile, and walked toward her husband of nearly forty-five years. "Let's go make lunch," she said. "I think I'm hungry too."

✸✳✧✦

I shouldn't be so hard on her, but sometimes I feel like I don't even know her anymore. Pete shook his head as he spooned the lukewarm canned tomato soup into his mouth. *I never used to have to ask her for crackers—she just knew. And she always made the soup nice and hot, the way I like it. Why would she stop doing that? Is she purposely trying to annoy me?*

Pete considered asking her—again—but she would no doubt feign innocence, as she had the last few times he asked why she hadn't done something for him. He sighed and pushed himself back from the table, then grabbed his walker and stood up.

"Where are you going?" Rachel asked with a hint of alarm in her voice. "Are you okay?"

"Of course I'm okay," he answered gruffly. "I want crackers for my soup, that's all. And apparently you're not going to get them for me. Are we out of them?"

Rachel frowned. "I don't know." She stood up. "I don't think so, but I'll look."

"Forget it. I'm already up. I can do it myself."

He steered his walker toward the cupboard and heard Rachel sigh as he sensed her plunking back down in her chair. The thought crossed his mind to apologize for being so short with her. Then again, why should he? Not like he'd asked her for a million dollars; he just wanted crackers with his soup, the way he'd eaten soup for as long as he could remember. How frustrating to have to ask her about such ridiculously familiar and simple things.

When he opened the cupboard, he had to move a few cartons and cans around before he found the crackers. Even then the box felt awfully light. "We're almost out," he groused. "You'd better buy some next time you go to the store."

He sat down and began to crumble the few stale crackers he'd found in the box, then dropped them into his soup. *Which probably isn't even warm anymore.* He shook his head and spooned a bite into his mouth, then nearly spit it back out.

"The crackers are stale, and the soup is almost cold. Good grief, Rachel, it's not like you were cooking a five-course meal; I just wanted a simple lunch. Can't you even do that for me anymore?"

Tears popped into her brown eyes, tugging at his heart. But he couldn't let go. The more he ignored these little slip-ups of hers, the worse the situation seemed to become. What in the world was wrong with her?

He opened his mouth to ask that very question; but before he could, she burst into tears and buried her face in her napkin. The waterworks were happening a lot more these days. If there was one thing Pete couldn't stand, it was seeing Rachel cry.

Disgusted, he rose from the table and pushed his walker into the TV room. Plopping down in his favorite chair, directly in front of the television, he snatched his cellphone from the end table where he'd left it and dialed the only nearby Chinese restaurant that delivered. Since he'd called them so often lately, he should put them on speed-dial. The thought didn't improve his mood any. He even imagined they recognized his number on their caller ID. But what was the alternative? Eating cold soup and stale crackers? Putting up with a wife who could no longer perform the most basic of household chores?

He sighed as he gave his order and heard the woman on the other end of the call say his food would be delivered in about thirty minutes.

He clicked off his phone and picked up the TV remote. At least he could watch some news while he waited.

✳✸✧⟡

I'm not very hungry, but I don't want to hurt Pete's feelings. He went to all the trouble of ordering Chinese food—even my favorite sweet-and-sour chicken—so the least I can do is sit down and have some with him. I don't know why we can't eat at the kitchen table, though. I really don't like listening to the news while we eat. It's never good news, and it gives me a headache.

Sitting in the rocker next to Pete's recliner, Rachel took a bite of rice. *Dry.* "Did they send any soy sauce?"

Pete turned from the TV to look at Rachel and frowned. "Sure they did. No thanks to you." He snatched up a small packet of the dark sauce and tossed it toward Rachel's TV tray, even though the tray was only a couple of feet away and he could easily have handed it to her.

Why does he always have to be so grouchy? I know the accident affected him, but he doesn't need to take out his anger on me all the time. She sighed. *Then again, why shouldn't he? It was my fault.*

She bent to retrieve the packet of sauce that had landed on the carpet, just inches from her tray. Struggling to get the packet open, she considered asking Pete for help but thought better of the idea. Finally able to tear off one corner, she tried to squeeze the soy sauce onto her rice, squirting some onto the sleeve of her white sweater.

Distressed, she pushed the tray back, stood up, and started to remove the stained garment.

"Now where are you going?"

Rachel stopped and looked at Pete, nervous at the level of annoyance she heard in his voice. For some reason, the sunlight from the window, reflecting off Pete's nearly bald head, distracted her. Determined to stay focused, she said, "I have to wash this." She held out her arm to show him the spot on her sleeve.

He shook his head, obviously irritated. "You're worse than a kid these days. Always forgetting stuff and spilling things." His frown deepened. "You need to pull yourself together, Rachel, you hear me? Things are getting ridiculous around here. You're supposed to be helping me, but you're just making my life harder."

Tears bit her eyes, and she turned from him. "I'm sorry, Pete. I'm doing the best I can." Without waiting for a reply, she headed for the laundry room to see if she could get the stain out of her favorite sweater.

Chapter 2

For some reason she couldn't identify, the Halloween decorations annoyed her. They were everywhere—lining the streets of otherwise quiet, respectable neighborhoods, and now at the mall besides.

Rachel shook her head, as she grabbed her purse and opened the car door. Maybe she was just getting too old to appreciate what used to be a pleasure for her. *When Lilly was little. When she still followed me everywhere and insisted we do everything together.*

A smile tugged at her lips, dispelling the agitation she'd felt since leaving home to do some much-needed shopping. *Lilly was so adorable then*, Rachel reminded herself, as she pushed into the chilly wind, wishing briefly she'd picked a nicer day to be out and about. *I don't know why Lilly felt she had to choose a college so far away. But at least she'll be home for the holidays soon.*

Thoughts of her only child always seemed to bolster her mood, and today was no exception. *Perhaps I can do a little early Christmas shopping while I'm here. I'd love to find a nice sweater for Lilly. As cold as it is today, it's so much worse back east where she is. But first I'd better get what I came here for.*

A prick of fear caused her to stop for a moment and try to remember exactly what she needed to buy, but then she shrugged and pressed on. With her purse slung over her shoulder and her keys tucked safely in her jacket pocket, she began to hum, "I'll Fly Away," the melody floating through her mind so often these days. By the time she stepped inside the temperature-controlled mall, her spirits were soaring again. She felt confident she'd remember what she needed when she saw the item. Until then, she'd simply window-shop her way around the mall, keeping a watchful eye for a special sweater for Lilly. Rachel smiled. And who knew? Maybe she'd even find something nice for Pete. *Lord knows he's been hard to please lately. I can't decide if I should try harder or just ignore him.*

She smiled as she passed through the food court, the smell of cinnamon and pizza combining to make her mouth water. Once again she thought of the many times she had brought Lilly here over the years. When she was a child, Rachel knew exactly what her daughter would want to eat. "Hot dogs—with lots of ketchup!" The child's words echoed in Rachel's mind, as clearly as if Lilly were standing beside her now, pulling on her hand and insisting she was hungry.

Hot dogs and ketchup. Rachel shook her head, her lips pulling into a broader smile. Lilly was in her early teens by the time she agreed to avail herself of the food court's many choices and try something else.

But by then she didn't want to come to the mall with me anymore. Rachel felt her smile fade. She'd known even back then her daughter's resistance was just a phase. Still, the thought Lilly preferred to shop with her friends instead of her mother saddened Rachel. *But Lilly's over that by now ... off at college, studying to become ...*

Rachel's frowned. What was Lilly studying? *A mother should remember.* Did her only child plan to become a doctor? A teacher? A scientist? Rachel shook her head, hoping the movement would clear away her confusion. *You'd think I could remember something as simple as my daughter's college major. What in the world is wrong with me these days?*

A stab of fear threatened to derail her entire shopping venture, but she clenched her jaw and pushed the dread away. She came here to find a sweater for Lilly, and she was bound and determined not to leave until she'd done so.

"Hey, Dad, it's me."

Lilly's cellphone sat on the table in front of her, speaker on. She'd been pleasantly surprised when her father answered the phone. Most of the time her calls home consisted of conversations with her mother, who always made excuses about why her father couldn't come to the phone. In fact, Lilly had tried her mom's cell number first. Since the call went to voice mail, she called the home phone instead. Hence, her conversation with her dad.

"So how are you?" she asked, pausing to take a sip of hot tea. She felt cold all the way to her bones, and she hoped a hot drink might help her warm up a bit.

"Okay," he answered.

Lilly could almost see him shrug. She knew if their conversation was going to gain any ground, she would have to take the initiative. "So, what have you been up to, Dad?"

"Not much."

Lilly sighed. She loved her father, but he had become so uncommunicative since the accident. She missed the laughing, outgoing man he'd been before, wishing he would someday find his way back to them. Still, she might as well accept the fact their dialogue was going nowhere. Her mother sounded a little flighty or confused at times, but at least she was able to maintain a two-way discussion—a lot more than she could say for her father.

"Um ... can I talk to Mom?"

"She's not here."

Lilly frowned. If she was out somewhere, why hadn't she answered her cell? "So ... where is she?"

"I don't know. Been looking for her, but I can't find her. And it's almost lunchtime."

Uh-oh. Dad was becoming more grouchy these days, sometimes over nothing in particular, but definitely over not being fed when he thought it was time.

"Listen, Dad, are you sure she's not out in the garage or the yard, or maybe even up in the attic, going through boxes of decorations? The holidays are coming, and she might be trying to get a head start on decorating. Besides, you know Mom doesn't just take off without telling you."

"She does lately. And I don't like it."

Of course, Dad worried about Mom. Since the accident, he expected his wife to be available to take care of his every need. Mom had even quit her job to stay home and take care of him fulltime, which had put a financial strain on them on top of everything else. Her parents needed the income, especially since her father had only been awarded partial disability after the accident, leaving him even more disgruntled and bitter. He never stopped maintaining he deserved full disability and believed he'd been cheated somehow. He blamed Mom for that as well. Lilly didn't think much of his attitude or of their post-accident situation in general, but Mom insisted she didn't mind. "It's the least I can do," she'd keep saying, "considering ..."

Pulling herself back to the present, Lilly sighed. "All right, Dad. Well, I'm sure she'll be back any minute, so please tell her I called, will you?"

"Okay."

The phone clicked off. *What? Not even a goodbye?* She shook her head. How did her mother put up with his attitude? Mom, at nearly twice Lilly's age, kept herself healthy and fit; but how could she continue to do so if her entire life had to revolve around Dad's needs and moods?

Lilly finished her tea and got up to take the cup to the sink. As she rinsed it, she noticed, as she had so often lately, how empty her sink was these days. Since Jacob left, everything seemed empty, with little hope the emptiness would go away anytime soon.

Blinking back the hot tears suddenly pricking her eyes, she turned from the sink and headed for her home office. She didn't have time for another crying jag. Crying wouldn't fix anything. Besides, there was work to be done.

Rachel sat at a small table at the food court, picking at a slice of pepperoni pizza. She was pleased with the sweater she'd found and knew Lilly would be as well. The soft peach color would be perfect with her daughter's warm brown eyes and creamy complexion. Lilly was a beauty, all right. Always had been. Rachel imagined the young men at college were fighting for her attentions.

Be picky, Lilly. Don't settle for second best. Of course, Lilly couldn't hear these thoughts. But talking to her daughter, sometimes silently and sometimes aloud, helped Rachel feel closer to Lilly. *I just wish you weren't so far away.* Rachel smiled then, as she remembered Christmas would arrive in just a couple of months. Lilly would be home from college, and the two of them would have so much to share.

Rachel sipped her small lemonade, washing down the spicy pizza that was barely warm and only slightly edible. *The pizza here used to be so much better. I almost always had a slice while Lilly ate her hot dog.* Rachel sighed. *I guess nothing stays the same forever.*

Deciding she might as well toss the pizza and head home, she got up and dropped her leftovers in the trash, then walked from the mall to the parking lot, clutching the bag with the peach-colored sweater she couldn't wait to give to Lilly. *Should I mail it to her or wait until she comes home for the holidays?*

The wind blew even colder than before, and the dark clouds looked threatening, as Rachel mulled over the question and hurried to the parking lot. Where was the car ... this section or the one to the right?

She stopped and looked as far as she could see in each direction. There were countless gray sedans, nearly all of which looked like her five-year-old Toyota Corolla. A hint of panic stirred in her stomach, and she was glad she hadn't eaten anymore of that stale pizza. She imagined she would have had a hard time keeping it down if she had.

"My car," she whispered. "Where is my car?"

Grabbing her keys from her jacket pocket, she repeatedly pressed the unlock button, while making her way up and down the rows of parked cars. No resounding chirp helped her hone in on her vehicle. Each time she thought she'd spotted the car, she'd get closer and realize it wasn't hers after all.

"Are you okay?"

The voice came from behind, to her right. She turned and spotted a tall young man with a heavy mustache, his brow furrowed as if worried. "Can I help you?" he asked.

Her mouth went dry, and she tried to quell the rising, unreasonable fear. *The man just wants to help.* But her racing heart refused to believe he meant to be kind.

"No," she said, clutching her keys more tightly. "I don't need any help."

He reached toward her, opening his mouth as if to speak. She ran off before he could say another word. She didn't want his help—didn't need it. She could find her car on her own. After all, she's the one who'd parked it. Who else would know where it was?

Running down yet another aisle, pressing her unlock button, the welcomed chirp finally stopped her in her tracks. *There it is.* Her car was just a few feet away, exactly where she'd left it.

"Oh, thank you, God," she said aloud, hurrying to the driver's door and pulling it open. She tossed her purse and the package inside, strapped herself in with the seatbelt, and started the car, hesitating before putting it into reverse.

Tears trickled down her cheeks as she clutched the steering wheel with both hands. "Thank you, God, for letting me find my car," she sobbed. "But what happened? I never used to forget where I put things. Why did I forget where I parked?"

Snagging a tissue from her purse, she wiped her eyes and blew her nose, taking deep breaths to help her stop crying. At last, determined to drive home where she would feel safe, she put the car in reverse and looked over her shoulder. As she backed out, she worried about Pete who was no doubt hungry by now. She needed to get home and fix him something to eat. He got so crabby when he was hungry.

Chapter 3

Rachel pulled into the garage, wondering briefly where she'd been and why she couldn't remember. She pushed the thought away as she turned off the engine.

She opened the car door and started to get out, then grabbed her purse and spotted the bag next to it. She frowned. *What's this? Did I stop and buy something while I was out?*

She opened the bag and peered inside. Pulling the soft sweater from the bag, she smiled. *Of course! A sweater for Lilly. And it's perfect. I wonder if I stopped to buy groceries too. I'm pretty sure I needed to.*

Using her key fob to open the trunk, she walked around to the back of the car, ready to unload her groceries. The trunk was empty, except for the umbrella and the first-aid kit she always kept there.

That's strange. Did I put the groceries in the back seat?

She closed the trunk and opened the car's back door. Nothing.

She sighed. Apparently she hadn't stopped to buy groceries after all. Did this mean they hadn't really needed any … or had she simply forgotten to get them?

Her ears began to ring, and she felt lightheaded. How was this possible? Had she perhaps stopped at the store, bought the groceries, and then forgotten to transfer them from the cart to her car? If that was the case, would the groceries still be there in the cart, waiting for her, if she returned to the store?

The hot, familiar tears bit her eyes again as she shook her head, trying desperately to clear her thoughts. She glanced at her watch. Nearly two in the afternoon. Pete would not be happy that she'd come home without groceries, especially if she'd forgotten to leave him some lunch. She couldn't remember if she had or not, but a growing sense of alarm told her she most likely hadn't.

She took deep breaths and stepped toward the door leading to the laundry room and then the kitchen. Maybe she could let herself in without Pete's noticing, then she'd find something to make him a quick lunch before he even realized she'd been gone.

Somewhat hopeful, she swallowed the lump in her throat, opened the door, stepped inside, and walked past the washer and dryer to the kitchen doorway. Her hopes were dashed before she could take another step. A nearly empty loaf of white bread lay open on the table, next to a partial jar of mayonnaise and an opened package of baloney. So much for her chance to fix lunch and avert a scene.

The tears trickled down her cheeks, and she felt as if she couldn't move. Sinking down to the cold linoleum floor, she grasped her purse in one hand and the package with Lilly's sweater in the other, while she sobbed and wondered what in the world she would tell Pete.

Pete was parked in front of the TV, eating his sandwich and occasionally glancing out the picture window, hoping his wife's gray Corolla would come into view. His annoyance at her leaving without telling him had grown throughout the four hours of her absence, but his concern for her safety was quickly becoming a factor as well.

What would he do if something happened to her? She might be getting a lot more forgetful, but at least she was there—most of the time anyway—to help him through the day. Until recently, she'd always taken care of everything, including the house, the bills, the taxes, the cooking, the laundry. How was he supposed to take care of himself if she wasn't around to do all those things?

When the car pulled into the driveway, he breathed a sigh of relief. She was all right, and she was home. His relief quickly changed to anger, however, as he considered how thoughtless she'd become. She should have told him she was going somewhere and when she'd be home and should have fixed lunch for him before she left.

He started to push the TV tray away to go confront her as she came in from the garage, but he stopped. No. He would make her come to him. Why should he interrupt his lunch, as awful as it was, when she was the one who'd caused the entire problem?

He shook his head, as a brief memory of their early days together flitted through his mind. She'd been a good wife then, but now? He'd thought she was trying to make up for what he'd lost in the accident—which was, after all, her fault—but lately he wasn't so sure. At times he recognized the attractive, sweet-natured woman she'd once been. But that person seemed to be disappearing behind someone Pete didn't know ... and didn't especially want to know.

He heard the laundry room door open, and he waited for her to come looking for him. But she didn't come, and soon he heard sobs coming from the kitchen.

What in the world ...?

With visions of her having fallen and hurt herself, he pushed his walker faster than usual, hoping he wasn't going to discover he had an invalid for a wife. That was all he needed.

When he reached the kitchen, he stopped in the doorway, staring at the crumpled figure on the floor, weeping as if the world were coming to an end. Nearly forty-five years of marriage or not, if he weren't dependent on the metal walker he leaned on at that very moment, he'd go right back to his TV and his lunch and ignore her all together.

But of course he couldn't do that. He needed her to survive, to pull out of the strange moods she'd been in lately. He'd have to try and find out what was wrong and what, if anything, he could do to help.

Gritting his teeth, he pushed his walker ahead of him and crossed the room to stop beside a sobbing Rachel, who had yet to look up and acknowledge his presence. He started to speak, then realized he had no idea what to say. Could the day—his life, for that matter—possibly get any worse?

Lilly pulled into her parents' driveway just hours after her father's phone call. The fact he had called at all set off alarm bells. When he told her he thought her mother was losing her mind, she didn't know what to think.

"I'll be there as soon as I can, Dad," she'd told him, then hung up and threw a few things in an overnight bag. Since she lived a couple hundred miles from her parents' home in the relatively small Southwest Washington Columbia River town of Camas, she'd decided she might as well bring what she needed for at least an overnight visit.

Coming home didn't appeal to her as it once had. Lilly had been close to her parents, particularly her mother, before the accident, before things had deteriorated.

The accident had become the dividing line of their lives—the good years before, the not-so-good years since. Would the line be there forever? With all her heart, she hoped it would not.

She'd been an only child and still had her key to the house where she'd grown up. She let herself in. "Mom? Dad?" She closed the door behind her and called out again as she made her way toward the kitchen. "Dad, I'm here. Mom? Where are you? Are you all right?"

The kitchen was dark, so she flipped on a light. Other than the evidence of a sandwich having been made earlier, Lilly could see no sign of anything having been cooked or eaten recently, so she turned around and proceeded down the hall toward the bedrooms.

She knocked on the door to her parents' room first, hoping she would find them both sleeping and well. Her father's grunt, which sounded somewhat like "come in," was the only response. She opened the door to find the room as dark as the kitchen had been.

"You two asleep already?" she whispered. "I'm sorry if I woke you."

"You didn't," her father said. "And turn on the light, will you? It's dark in here."

The obvious retorts to his comment surfaced quickly, but she quashed them. No sense complicating an already difficult situation. When she flipped the light, Dad lay in bed alone, a couple of car magazines beside him. "Dad, where's Mom?"

Dad glowered. "It's nice to see you too, daughter."

"I'm sorry." She stepped toward the bed and bent down to give her father a hug, wrinkling her nose at the odor that greeted her. Apparently he hadn't bothered to shower for a day or two. "How are you, Dad? And where's Mom?"

"She's in the guest room," he answered. "At least, that's where she was when I came in here. Who knows? Maybe she's taken off on another mystery ride, like she did this morning."

Lilly stood up and frowned. "What do you mean, a mystery ride? Where did she go?"

Still lying flat, her father shrugged. "Who knows? I sure don't. I asked her, but she doesn't seem to know either.

I thought maybe she'd gone to the grocery store—which would have been nice, since we hardly have anything to eat around here—but she didn't have any groceries when she came inside, and I didn't find any in the car either."

Lilly didn't much like her father's report. Things were not as they should be. She made a mental note to pick up some food in the morning. "I'm going to go check on Mom. I'll be back."

When her father made no response, she turned and walked out and down the hall to the guestroom, passing her childhood bedroom. When she opened the door, she found that room was also dark. Didn't her parents believe in lights these days?

She flipped the switch, bathing the room in light. Her mother sat on the bed and squinted at the sudden brightness, her purse on one side and a bag on the other. As recognition dawned, she smiled.

"You came," she said. "I prayed you would, and here you are. Oh, thank you, Lord!"

Lilly walked toward the bed and sat down beside her mother. "Yes, as soon as Dad called and told me what was going on. He seemed concerned."

Mom raised her eyebrows. "Really?" She shrugged. "Well, if he was, I doubt he was worried about me."

There was no diplomatic way to answer. Best to ignore the sarcasm. "Mom, what happened today? And why are you sitting here in the dark? I don't understand any of this."

Her mother's voice dropped to a near whisper. "Neither do I, sweetheart. And I don't know what to do about it."

Before Lilly could say anything, tears began to trickle down her mother's cheeks.

"Oh, Mama," Lilly took in a deep breath, pulled her mother into a hug, then stroked her hair and whispered words of comfort, none of which seemed to do any good. Her mother's tears wet Lilly's blouse as they huddled together on the bed in the guestroom, which her mother referred to as her "retro-room." What in the world was going on here?

Lilly decided she would indeed spend the night and then first thing in the morning, she was going to call her mother's pastor to ask for advice. She might even invite him to come over and assess the situation for himself, though Dad wouldn't want the pastor to visit.

Chapter 4

Rachel awoke with a start. The sweater! She'd forgotten to give Lilly the sweater ... or had she? Suddenly, she wasn't so sure. Maybe she had and just didn't remember. And was Lilly still there, or had she gone back to school? What was she doing home anyway? It wasn't the holidays yet ... was it?

She sat up and flipped on the lamp beside her bed, eliciting an almost immediate groan from Pete.

"What in the world ...?" He rose on one elbow and scowled, even as he squinted at the light. "Rachel, what are you doing? It's the middle of the night!"

Rachel frowned. Was it really the middle of the night? And what night would that be? She had such difficulty keeping track of time lately.

"Is it Monday or Tuesday?" she asked.

Pete shook his head. "It's Saturday," he growled. "And what difference does that make?" He glanced at his watch. "Good grief, Rachel. It's two-thirty in the morning! Is there a reason you turned the light on? Is something wrong?"

Two-thirty in the morning? That meant if Lilly had spent the night, she was still here. "That's a relief," she said aloud. "And no, there's nothing wrong—not really. I just woke up and realized I didn't give Lilly her sweater— at least, I don't think I did." She threw back the covers and dropped her legs over the side of the bed. She had her slippers on before Pete spoke again.

"What are you talking about? What sweater?"

"The one I bought her yesterday." She turned back to her husband. "Or was it earlier than that?" She shrugged. "I can't remember, but I'm almost sure I didn't give it to her." She reached for her faded blue robe, draped over the foot of her side of the bed. "I'm going to go see if it's in the kitchen or living room. If not, then I must have given it to her already."

Pete opened his mouth as if he were going to say something ... then chomped down and shook his head. "Fine. Go look for the sweater. But whether you find it or not, don't go looking in Lilly's room. There's no sense waking her up too."

So Lilly had spent the night after all. Rachel smiled. "Thank you, Pete. I'll be right back."

Pete sighed and laid his head back on the pillow. Rachel imagined he'd be asleep again before she returned. *That man has always been able to fall asleep on a dime.* A slight chuckle escaped as she left the bedroom.

✡ ❄ ✦ ✧

"I heard voices," Lilly said, stepping out of her room and coming face to face with her mother in the hallway. "Is everything okay?"

Mom appeared pleased. "I'm so glad you're still here, sweetheart. I was afraid you might have gone back to school already, and I didn't have a chance to give you your sweater."

Lilly took a deep breath. Her mother seemed even more confused now than when she'd found her in the guest room earlier.

"Mom," she said, taking her arm and attempting to turn her around, "you need to go back to bed. We can talk about this in the morning."

Mom shook her head. "Your sweater," she insisted. "I have to find your sweater and give it to you before I can go back to sleep."

"Mom, please, you gave it to me before we went to bed. Don't you remember?"

The look on her mother's face was answer enough; she didn't remember although she was obviously relieved to know Lilly had the sweater. Mom's expression changed to concern. "Did you like it? Did it fit?"

Lilly's heart twisted at the anxiety she saw in her mother's brown eyes. Her short, reddish-brown hair stuck straight up in back, somehow accentuating the gray strands framing her face. Pulling her into a hug, Lilly said, "It fit perfectly. And I loved it, Mom. I love everything you give me, and that beautiful sweater is no exception. The color is perfect for me."

Rachel pulled back and a satisfied grin spread across her face. "I knew it. I knew the minute I saw that sweater, it had your name on it."

"You're right, Mama," Lilly said tenderly, reverting to the name she'd called her mother years earlier. "It definitely has my name on it. And I like it so much I'll wear it tomorrow. How does that sound?"

"Perfect!" Mom reached up and patted the side of Lilly's face. "You're a good daughter, and I'm so happy you're doing well in school. You'll be graduating before you know it." Her face sobered. "I just hope, when you do, you find a job closer to home. I don't like having you so far away. I never could understand why you couldn't go to a college here in Oregon—or at least on the West Coast. It isn't like there aren't any good ones here, you know."

Lilly exerted every drop of will power she had to blink back the tears that stung her eyes. "You're right, Mom. But I'm home for a visit now, so let's go back to bed and try to get some sleep. We can talk about all this in the morning."

"Yes, we can talk at breakfast. I'm going to make you your favorite pancakes."

"Sounds delicious, Mom." Lilly opened her parents' bedroom door and stood back as her mother entered. "Turn out the light and go to bed now. I'll see you in the morning."

A quick glance told Lilly her dad was still awake and no doubt annoyed at being so, even as he flipped through the pages of one of his car magazines. Ah well, his ongoing bad mood wasn't something she could fix in the middle of the night—or anytime, for that matter.

She closed her parents' door and turned to go back to her own room, reminding herself to get groceries first thing in the morning—including the ingredients for pancakes.

Lilly's three-day visit had been wonderful, though Rachel wished her daughter could have stayed longer. She understood—Lilly needed to get back to school and was surprised she had been able to come at all before the Thanksgiving and Christmas breaks. Rachel was already looking forward to her daughter's return for both holidays.

"I miss her," Rachel commented, as she and Pete sat at the breakfast table, finishing their last cup of coffee. Lilly had insisted on doing all the cooking while she was here, and she had made breakfast earlier in the morning, just before leaving.

Pete grunted an answer without looking up from his newspaper.

He reads that thing religiously every morning; I just wish he'd spend half as much time reading the Bible Lilly bought him a few years ago.

Rachel frowned. How long ago was that, anyway? She had the hardest time keeping dates in any sort of order these days.

A prick of conscience brought her back to her previous thought, and she cringed at the guilt that engulfed her.

How can I expect Pete to read his Bible when he scarcely ever sees me reading mine anymore?

"I'll be right back," she said, rising from the table.

Pete looked up from his paper. "Where are you going?"

Aha. So he was paying attention to her after all.

"You'll see." She left the kitchen and headed to their bedroom, where she retrieved her once well-read Bible from the bottom shelf of the nightstand next to her side of the bed. The twinge of conscience intensified when she saw the dust that had collected on the beloved book. How long had it been sitting there, untouched?

She stroked the leather cover, admiring the gold letters that spelled her name. "Rachel Beckwith," she read aloud. "Well, Rachel Beckwith, you're going to start reading this book again—regularly—and going to church too." She'd never been as involved in church life as some of her acquaintances, but she'd always been so busy—working and taking care of everything at home, then quitting her job to take care of Pete. No wonder she scarcely had time to do anything beyond the absolute necessities.

She tried to stem the ebb and flow of guilt, reminding herself why she had not been as faithful in church attendance as she thought she should be. Her excuses didn't help much. With a sigh, she carried the Bible to the kitchen where Pete still sat, perusing his paper. He didn't even look up when she sat down beside him and opened to the middle and began reading the Psalms.

Chapter 5

Lilly called as soon as she got home, remembering her promise to let her mother know she'd arrived safely.

"Already?" Her mother sounded surprised. "What did you do, fly?"

Lilly smiled. "No, Mom, I didn't fly. I drove. But I did make good time. How are you and Dad doing?"

"All right, but ... Lilly, I still can't figure out how you drove nearly three thousand miles in a matter of hours."

Lilly sighed. Though she'd tried, both gently and persistently, to convince her mother she'd been out of college for several years—had, in fact, been married for five of those years and was now in the process of divorce—apparently Mom was still confused. Lilly bit her tongue and swallowed her words. If she hadn't been able to explain things to her mother during the three days she was there, she certainly wasn't going to be able to do so during a brief phone conversation.

"So what are you and Dad going to do for the rest of the day?" she asked, keeping her voice light and positive. "Got any plans? The weather looked good when I left this morning. Why don't the two of you go out somewhere special for lunch?"

Lilly held her breath, as her mom paused before answering. "I don't think so, sweetheart. We don't go out much these days."

That's an understatement. Aloud, she said, "Well, then, maybe you should. Maybe that's exactly what the two of you should do."

After another pause, her mother spoke. "Here's your dad. I need to go do something."

Lilly pulled the cellphone from her ear and frowned at it. What in the world did her mother need to do that couldn't wait until they finished their conversation?

"Hello." Her father's voice was gruff, but his words were caring. "Did you make it home okay?"

"I did. And I wanted to make sure you two are okay. I've been trying to talk Mom into the two of you going out somewhere—to lunch, maybe."

"We're fine. Same as always, I guess."

Lilly wasn't surprised Dad ignored her suggestion. "That's good. I'm glad." Seems her conversations with her father couldn't transcend the very basic, whether on the phone or in person.

"There is one thing, though."

Was Dad actually offering information, something beyond short, direct answers to her questions? "What's that, Dad?"

"She was reading her Bible at breakfast this morning."

And that was worth mentioning because ...? "Mom always reads her Bible ... doesn't she?" But even as Lilly voiced the question, she realized she hadn't seen her mother with her Bible the last few days.

"Not lately."

"So today is the first time in a while, then."

"Yep."

"Well ... that's good, right?"

"I guess. She even said something about going back to church."

Now this was surprising information—not because Mom was considering going *back* to church—rather, she hadn't been attending in the first place. Lilly chided herself for not following up on her thought to call the pastor. She couldn't remember a time her mother had missed church, at least not by choice. How long had this been going on? Then she realized she might have known if she and her mother discussed such things. "How long has she not been going?"

Lilly imagined her father shrugging as he answered. "I don't know. A month or two, maybe ... or more. Probably more."

Hmm ... Mom had cut back on her activities, even quitting her job at the bank after the accident, but Lilly hadn't realized things had become this bad. Could this be at least one of the reasons her mother seemed to be withdrawing lately? With a lack of social interaction and no one but Dad to talk to...

Lilly sighed. "What about Mom's women's group, the one that meets once a month?"

"What group? I don't know anything about a group."

"Yes, you do, Dad. I think it's the Red Hat club, or something like that. Don't you remember? Mom told me about it a few years ago—said one of the neighbors invited her, and they went together. She really seemed to enjoy it."

Silence.

Okay, fine. It's obvious I'm not going to get anywhere this way. Maybe I should contact Mom's pastor after all, or a couple of the neighbors, if I can remember their names.

"I gotta go." Her dad's terse statement interrupted Lilly's thoughts.

"Okay, Dad. Tell Mom I'll call her in a day or two."

"Why?"

What kind of question was that? "To check on her, of course."

"Okay. Bye."

"Bye, Dad."

Lilly ended the call, then laid her phone on the kitchen counter. Things were definitely not okay at home, and apparently she'd be the one who'd have to figure out why—and what to do about the problems.

✳ ✽ ✧ ✦

"Pete, have you seen my keys?"

It was just after ten on Sunday morning, and Pete was sitting in his chair in front of the TV, watching football and sipping his third cup of coffee. *Even though I had to ask her to remake it,* he reminded himself, as he set the now nearly empty coffee mug on the TV tray next to his chair, *since she forgot to put the coffee in the first time. Brought me a mug of hot water.* He sighed and shook his head. So was it up to him to remember everything now? How would he know where she left the car keys? He hadn't driven anywhere since ...

"I don't know, Rachel. Aren't they hanging on the hook by the back door? That's where you always insisted I put them when I was still driving."

As if she hadn't thought of that possibility before, Rachel turned and walked toward the laundry room where they regularly hung their keys by the door. Pete once again shook his head and went back to watching his game.

In moments, she was back, looking confused but also surprisingly attractive. He wondered why he hadn't noticed how pretty she looked until now. "New dress?"

She frowned, obviously puzzled by his question, then glanced down at what she wore. "No," she said, raising her head. "I don't think so. But I want to wear it to church today."

So she'd decided to go back to church after all. Good for her. He just hoped she didn't start pushing for him to go with her. He and God hadn't seen eye to eye in a while now—if, indeed, they ever had—and he expected their relationship wouldn't change anytime soon. "Will you be back in time to make me lunch?"

"I ... I guess so. First, I have to find my keys."

"Didn't you just check the key hook to see if they were there? You always put them there."

She shook her head. "Not this time. And they weren't there when I looked earlier this morning either. I just can't figure out why."

He wanted to scold her for being so careless with the car keys, but thought better of saying anything. Whether she found the keys or not, he wished she'd let him watch TV in peace—and, of course, be home in time to make lunch before the first game ended and the next one started.

A snack while I wait for lunch wouldn't be a bad idea. He thought he'd ask Rachel to bring him something; but she'd already disappeared, no doubt still looking for the elusive keys. Heaving himself up from the chair and onto the walker, he scooted into the kitchen and opened the refrigerator. A lone piece of coffee cake rested in the otherwise empty package on the top shelf. Deciding it would be perfect for a mid-morning snack while he finished the last of his coffee, he pulled it out, wondering if it was worth the bother to warm it in the microwave.

Before he could decide, Rachel joined him in the kitchen, still fussing about the keys. He wasn't happy to see tears in her eyes. *I'm not up to another one of her crying jags.* He started back toward the TV room.

"Here they are!"

His wife's elated cry stopped him in his tracks. When he turned, she stood in front of an open cupboard, triumphantly holding up her keys.

"Where were they?"

"Right here," she said, pointing toward the shelf that contained the coffee.

He wanted to ask her why she'd put them there, but he decided asking took more effort than ignoring the obvious. She no doubt had them in her hand earlier when he pointed out her first pot of coffee contained nothing more than hot water. When she made a new pot—this one including the coffee grounds—she'd obviously laid them down on the shelf when she took out the coffee can.

Another mystery solved. He settled back into his chair in time to see his favorite quarterback throw a completion on a third down. As he took a bite of the cold, stale coffee cake, all thoughts of Rachel and her forgetfulness faded.

Rachel was relieved. She'd been a bit confused when she first left the house, momentarily forgetting which direction to turn to head for the church. Had it been that long since she'd gone? She'd have to be careful not to let that happen again.

Thankfully, she'd chosen correctly and soon ended up in front of the church. *Funny.* She glanced at her watch as she pulled into the parking lot. *The eleven o'clock service should start in ten minutes. Where is everybody?*

Only a few cars dotted the otherwise empty lot, and even those began to disappear as people came from the direction of the church's front doors, climbed into their vehicles, and drove away. She glanced at her watch again, then grabbed her Bible and exited her car, heading for the front of the building. The church doors were open, so she stepped through them into the foyer, where a handful of people milled about. Looking for someone she recognized, she breathed a sigh of relief when she spotted Pastor Dave.

"Pastor," she called out, heading in his direction, "where is everybody?"

The middle-aged pastor, dressed in gray slacks and a matching sports coat, smiled when he spotted her.

"Rachel! I'm so glad to see you. We've missed you."

A familiar stab of guilt pierced her heart once again. "I know. I should have come sooner—or called." She shook her head. "I ... I'm not sure why I didn't."

Pastor Dave put his hand on her shoulder. "You're here now; that's what matters. Though I do wish you'd gotten here in time for the service."

Rachel trembled. *The service is over?* "You mean ... I'm too late?"

The pastor's smile faded a bit. "I'm afraid so, Rachel. Did you forget we meet at nine-thirty now?"

Rachel's cheeks heated. "I guess I did. I thought the service was at eleven."

Dark eyes registered something Rachel couldn't quite define, then softened with what appeared to be concern. "Rachel, we haven't had an eleven o'clock service here in years. Only the one at nine-thirty. Don't you remember?"

She didn't, but she wasn't about to admit she'd forgotten. "Of course," she mumbled, forcing a smile. "I think maybe I just got ... confused or something. I've been busy, you know ... very busy, taking care of Pete and all. Sometimes, I ... forget things."

"I understand." Pastor Dave nodded, as if to emphasize his statement. "Rachel, why don't we go find a seat in the sanctuary? I imagine it's empty by now. We can talk ... or pray ... if you'd like."

Rachel shook her head. "No. No, I can't. I ... I need to get back to Pete. I don't like to leave him alone, you know."

Before he could say another word, Rachel turned and headed for the door, tears biting her eyes. What was wrong with her? Why couldn't she remember the simplest of things? And what was going to happen to her and Pete if her memory continued to fail her?

Chapter 6

Rachel hadn't meant to catch the old road out of town but found herself there when she stopped thinking about what had happened at church. She looked in all directions, trying to get her bearings. Nothing seemed to register until she saw the highway marker.

"I'm headed for the beach," she said aloud. "How did I end up here?" She shook her head. *I don't want to go to the beach. I have so much to do at home, and I know Pete's waiting for me.* Hot tears threatened, but she blinked them back. *I should never have come out today. I was safe at home where I could have made Pete's lunch and had a nice, quiet day. Instead, here I am, going somewhere I don't want to be.*

Her eyes darted from left to right and back again, continuing to take in her surroundings. Another sign came into view, reminding her of something she'd known for years. Yet it struck her now as if the sign had new information. *Forty-eight miles to the beach!* She glanced at her gas gauge. She probably had enough gas to get there, but what about the return trip? Would she be able to find a place to refuel? Would she remember how? If not, did she have her Triple-A card with her? Had she even bothered to renew her membership? Worse yet, if she continued to put more miles between herself and home, would she be able to find her way back at all?

I can't call Pete; he doesn't drive anymore. And besides, I think we only have one vehicle now—the one I'm driving. I just wish Lilly weren't so far away. I know she'd come and get me if she could. Then again, she can't just walk out of one of her classes to come and rescue me, especially since she's on the opposite side of the country.

Rachel slowed for a curve as the thought struck. *A police station might be a good place to stop. They could tell me how to get home again. I just wish I knew where there was one.*

A horn blasted as a car zipped past her in the opposite direction. The man in the driver's seat looked angry. Had she done something wrong, drifted over into his lane, perhaps?

I can't go any farther. I have to pull off the road … now.

She pulled into a wide space on the right, put the car into park, shut off the engine, and then grabbed the top of the steering wheel, laying her head on her hands. This time she didn't even try to hold back the tears.

✶✻✧✧

How much time had passed? Thirty minutes? Less? More? A rap on the driver-side window pulled Rachel back to the moment, as if from a dream. Where had she been? Where was she now?

She turned her head and saw a friendly-looking young man peering at her. "Auto club," he said through the closed window. "You called for help."

Rachel blinked and looked around. A white tow truck was parked behind her, though she was unable to see the truck's side, where she imagined the words were to confirm the identity of the man waiting for her to open the window.

"Ma'am, you called for help," he repeated. "Are you all right?"

I called for help? I don't remember calling anyone. Though I do remember thinking I should.

"I ... I'm sorry," she said, opening the door slightly, as the young man stepped backward. "I suppose I did call. Yes, I'm sure I did. Thank you for coming."

When she got out of the car and stood between the open door and the front seat, she glanced up and realized how tall the man was—and how young. *But then, nearly everyone seems young to me these days.* She also noticed his name stitched across the top of his left-hand shirt pocket—Gregory.

"You ... didn't specify what was wrong with your car when you called," Gregory said. "Do you think you might need a tow?"

She drew her brow together. Did she need a tow? No. She was certain she didn't. "I ... I don't think so."

Gregory paused for a moment, then said, "Um, Mrs. Beckwith, before I can look at your car and try to figure out what's wrong, I'll need to see your auto-club card and your driver's license."

"Oh, I—" She turned and reached into the front seat to retrieve her purse. She was relatively certain she had her driver's license, but not so certain about her auto-club card.

Rachel quickly located the driver's license and showed it to him. Gregory examined the card, then waited patiently as she fumbled through her wallet, hoping to find the one she was beginning to think she didn't have.

"At last!" A huge sigh of relief oozed as she spotted the card. "I hope it's still current," she said, her hand trembling as she handed it to him.

"It is," he said, smiling reassuringly. "Though you might want to renew it soon. It expires next month."

Thank God! And yes, it was obvious she would need to renew the card, especially if she continued to have these forgetful spells when she was out driving.

"All right," Gregory said, "let's see if we can figure out what's wrong with your car. Are you out of gas? Because if you are, I can put in enough to get you to the next gas station."

Rachel shook her head. "No. No, I don't believe I'm out of gas."

"Did your car just stop? Was it running rough, and you decided to pull off the road? Did one of your warning lights come on? I checked all your tires when I first pulled up, and they seem fine."

The enormity of trying to answer so many questions made her head hurt. "I ... I don't know what's wrong. I was late for church, and then I took the wrong road and ended up out here. I don't want to go to the beach. I want to go ... home." A sob escaped as she spoke the last word, then she eased back inside the car and slumped down into the driver's seat. "I just want to go home," she repeated, brushing at the unwelcome tears refusing to go away.

"It's all right, Mrs. Beckwith. We're going to get you home. But first we have to figure out what's wrong with the car."

She shook her head, slowly at first, then more forcefully as she remembered what had transpired just before she pulled off the road. "I'm sorry," she said, still swiping at her tears. "I probably shouldn't have called you. There's nothing wrong with my car. It ... it's me. There's something wrong with me, and I don't know what to do."

Looking into his sympathetic dark eyes, she said, "Please, help me get home. I just want to go home!"

Gregory nodded. "I understand," he said, his voice soothing. He glanced again at her driver's license. "Are you still at the same address ... on Fremont Lane?"

She was glad she at least remembered that much. "Yes. We—my husband and I—have been there for years. Our daughter too, but she's away right now. At college, I think."

"All right, Mrs. Beckwith, that's not really too far from here. Can I call your husband to come and get you?"

Rachel shook her head. "Oh, no," she said. "He can't come. He can't even drive. I have to take care of him, you know, since the accident ..."

"That's all right. Is there anyone else?"

Rachel tried desperately to think of someone, but even the few faces she pulled from her memory didn't have names she could recall. And she certainly didn't know their numbers. Were they saved in her cellphone? The thought of scrolling through the list of contacts and trying to identify someone made her stomach twist in a knot. "I'm afraid not. Can you take me?"

Gregory hesitated. "I ... no, I can't. At least, I shouldn't. I mean, it's not my job, but"—he took a deep breath—"I'll be off soon, and I need to head back to the office, so maybe"—he took another deep breath—"do you think you could follow me if I lead you home? You'd have to stop crying, of course. Can you do that? Can you calm down and follow me? Then I can go on from there."

Rachel swallowed. "Yes. Yes, I can do that. Thank you so much."

In less than twenty minutes, Rachel spotted her driveway and heaved a huge sigh of relief. She'd made it. She was home.

She waved an unseen goodbye and mouthed a silent thank you to the young man as his tow truck continued down the road. He honked and stuck his hand out the open window to wave goodbye, then signaled for a right turn, no doubt heading for the nearest main road.

Smiling, she hit the garage door opener on her sun visor and pulled inside. She imagined Pete would be annoyed she hadn't gotten back sooner, but she'd fix him something special to eat. Then everything would be all right again.

Pete was relieved when he heard the garage door open and Rachel's car pulling inside. *It's about time. I'm starving.*

He waited for his wife to come into the TV room and ask what he'd like for lunch. When she didn't show up, he sighed and pulled himself to his feet. *Maybe she just came as far as the kitchen and stopped to fix me something.*

Pete got to the kitchen doorway and stopped, leaning on his walker. As she stared at him from the opposite door, his eyes locked with hers. Apparently, this was as far as she'd made it from the garage. What in the world was she doing standing there? He was struck again at how nice she looked in her pinkish dress, but she looked as if she'd been crying.

"Are you ... okay?" Pete asked.

At the sound of his words, she seemed to shake herself out of some sort of trance, her face finally registering recognition.

"Pete," she said, stepping farther into the kitchen, "I know you're hungry. I would have come sooner, but ... I was late for church, and then I got lost ..."

Pete frowned. What was she talking about? How could she have gotten lost? The church was less than five miles away, and she'd driven there countless times—though not lately, he had to admit. He started to ask how she'd gotten lost, but Rachel stopped him.

"Never mind," she said, waving away anymore conversation on the matter. "I'll get lunch going right away. I'm hungry too. You go on back to your game, and I'll have everything ready in a jiffy."

He shook his head. There was no understanding that woman these days, no reasoning with her. He supposed he would simply have to be content to eat whatever she fixed and not expect anything more.

Turning his walker in the direction of the TV room, he shuffled off to wait for his wife and his food—and to watch the opening minutes of the next game.

Chapter 7

Dave Barnett had been the pastor of Wildflower Community Church for nearly ten years, and he truly loved his job. Going to Bible college immediately after high school seemed like the natural thing to do. After all, he was a pastor's kid and had always been a people person. The rest—as they say—was history.

As he sat behind his desk, he smiled and picked up his wife's picture placed between those of their two daughters, both teenagers now. Barbara's blue eyes and unruly black curls had captured his heart from the first time he laid eyes on her. If anything, he loved her even more now.

Our kids look just like you. His eyes darted from her picture to the two still sitting on the desk, then back again. *As I've told you many times, that's one more thing we can all be thankful for.* He chuckled as he replaced her photo.

As he nearly always did, Pastor Dave had taken Monday off to spend with his family. Since this was Tuesday, he needed to get to work. He had three appointments with parishioners today and a board meeting tonight and wanted to have all his ducks in a row before the meeting.

Disciplining himself to focus on his computer screen, he breathed a silent prayer for wisdom and guidance, then opened a new file, jotting down notes as thoughts came to him, much as he did when outlining a sermon.

He hadn't gotten far when the phone rang. He ignored the rings, assuming his assistant would answer. Apparently, she didn't. *Kelly must be away from her desk.* He picked up the receiver and said hello. He didn't recognize the woman's voice.

"Hello, Pastor Barnett. This is Lilly Grisham—Pete and Rachel Beckwith's daughter."

The light came on. "Lilly! Of course. So good to hear from you. How are you?" He paused a moment, wondering why she'd called, since he'd met her only a couple of times and hadn't seen her since one of the Mother's Day events at church. According to her mother, she'd attended Wildflower Community as a child, long before he came on staff.

His memory jogged suddenly to Rachel's odd behavior on Sunday morning. He knew Lilly didn't consider Wildflower Community her home church—in fact, he had no idea if she even had a home church at this point in her life. Was she calling because she had concerns about her mother?

"Is everything all right?" he asked.

"Sure," came a hesitant answer. From her tone, Dave suspected everything was definitely not all right.

"It's ... about my mother." Lilly paused before continuing. "Have you seen her lately? Talked with her?"

"As a matter of fact"—he paused momentarily to consider how he should answer—"I saw her Sunday morning, just after church let out."

He heard a note of relief in Lilly's voice. "So she was there. Good. My dad said he thought she might start attending again."

"Yes, she was here, though not for the service. What I mean is ... she missed the service. She got here just as everyone else was leaving."

Lilly didn't respond right away, so Dave waited—once again praying for wisdom. There was obviously something wrong, but he wasn't quite sure what.

At last Rachel's daughter spoke. "I'm worried about her. I think my dad is too. Things just aren't ... right with her. You know what I mean?"

Not really. "Can you be a bit more specific? I'm not sure I understand what you're saying."

Lilly's sigh seemed to echo before she spoke. "I'm not saying she has ... Alzheimer's or anything like that. Still, I think maybe—maybe she's having some memory issues. She seems confused much of the time and forgets things she would never have forgotten before. I know she's sixty-seven now, but ..."

Was Lilly waiting for him to respond? "Lilly, if I remember correctly, you live a few hours away. But would you like to come in and speak with me about this?"

"I ... yes, Pastor, I would. I think that might be a good idea. My schedule is relatively flexible right now. I'm subbing at the school and writing from home. Besides, going to Wildflower to see you would give me another opportunity to drop in on my parents again. I have a feeling I might have to start visiting more often in the very near future."

Pastor Dave put her on hold and buzzed his assistant, hoping she was back at her desk. She was, and she told him she would set up an appointment with Lilly Grisham for some time during the week. Relieved, he ended the call and went back to his notes for the board meeting.

The day had been unseasonably warm, and Rachel wanted to enjoy every last minute of it. As September turned to October and the days marched steadily on toward a long, gray, wet Pacific Northwest winter, she resolved to soak up every last minute of sunshine whenever she got the chance.

Rachel struggled to remember the date as she sat alone on the front-porch swing watching the sun's last rays spill over the horizon, one of the most peaceful moments she'd experienced in a while now. Though she couldn't seem to remember the date, she at least knew the day—Wednesday.

The front door squeaked open, and she looked up to see Pete pushing his walker ahead of him. A moment of surprise warmed her heart, as she wondered if he had actually come looking for her so they could spend some time together. Then she saw the scowl on his face.

"So here you are," he groused, carefully lowering himself onto the swing beside her.

She braced her feet on the porch to help keep the swing from flying backward and dumping them both onto the ground. When the two of them were settled, she spoke, deciding to ignore the accusatory tone of his voice. "Yes. It's been such a lovely day. I wasn't ready for it to end yet. So I decided to come out here and watch the sun go down."

Pete harrumphed. "Well, the least you could do is let me know when you're going outside. I looked all over for you in the house."

Rachel drew her brows together in a puzzled frown. He couldn't be hungry. They'd just finished dinner ... hadn't they? A slight feeling of panic stirred in her stomach. Had she only imagined they'd had dinner?

"I'm sorry," she said. "Did I forget something? Are you hungry?"

His scowl deepened. "How could I be hungry? We just finished dinner less than an hour ago." He shook his head, as if she'd asked the dumbest question ever.

Perhaps she had. But she was relieved to know she hadn't forgotten dinner. On the other hand, if he wasn't hungry, why had he been looking for her? He usually spent every evening in the TV room, tuned out to everything but "Jeopardy" and "Wheel of Fortune"—and, of course, a football game if there happened to be one. So what was on his mind?

He answered her question before she asked. "Lilly called. She wanted to talk to you, but I couldn't find you."

Rachel started to get to her feet. "Oh, I'll go talk to her right now."

Pete looked at her as if she'd just landed in a space ship. "Don't you think I'd have brought the phone out if she was still waiting to talk to you?" He shook his head again. "Honestly, Rachel, think once in a while, will you? Do you see the phone in my hand?"

She didn't, of course, but she decided to ignore his question, focusing instead on the fact Pete had answered the phone for a change. He rarely did anymore. He seemed to leave nearly everything for her to do. Was he starting to pick up the slack a little bit? With the way her memory had been lately, she would certainly welcome any help he might offer.

"So ... what did she have to say? Is everything okay?"

Pete shrugged. "Yeah, I guess so. We didn't talk long. She just said she was coming tomorrow to spend a couple of days."

Rachel's heart skipped a beat. How wonderful—Lilly was coming to visit. They hadn't seen each other since ... when? She tried to remember. Just before the fall semester started, she imagined.

"That's wonderful," she declared, a smile pulling at her lips. "I've missed her—though I did think she'd have to wait for the holidays before coming." She felt her smile fade. "I do hope everything's okay at school."

"She said she didn't have any teaching classes scheduled until next week, and she also said she'd bring her writing assignment with her."

Rachel's heart warmed again. "I'm so glad she's followed up on her writing. I always knew she'd be good at it. Did she say what she was writing about?"

"I didn't ask."

"Well, whatever her project is, I'm sure she'll get an A. She always does." Rachel laid her hand on Pete's arm.

"She's a good student, our Lilly. And a good girl too. I just pray she finds a good Christian man soon. She'll make someone a wonderful wife and mother."

Pete stiffened his back and turned his upper body, positioning himself to look at her more fully. "What are you talking about, Rachel? She's already been married, and that was a disaster. I'm just glad they didn't have any kids. What a mess that would be."

A sudden cool breeze seemed to shift the atmosphere as well as lower the temperature, and Rachel shivered. She had no idea how to respond to Pete. How could Lilly have been married? She was still in college ... wasn't she?

Rachel wrung her hands. Oh, if only she could remember the "next thing" so she could go do it, the way her mother had taught her. But she hadn't a clue what the next thing might be. Hot tears stung her eyes, and her heart began to race. She nearly jumped to her feet, not looking down at Pete as she hurried to the front door nor giving even one thought to the fact she might have overturned the porch swing and her husband along with it.

"I'm going inside," she announced. "It's getting cold out here."

Lilly had kept a close eye on the weather since the last few days of sunshine were just about over. A front was moving in, and the cold wind blasted her the minute she stepped out of her sleek red Mazda after parking in her parents' driveway. Dark clouds in the distance promised rain wasn't far behind.

I sure hope Dad remembered to tell Mom I was coming. She grabbed her purse, jacket, and overnight bag. *It's so unusual for him to answer the phone these days. He probably won't admit how worried he is about Mom.* Lilly sighed. *And so am I.*

She used her key to let herself in, then called out to her parents as she made her way to the kitchen. It was mid-morning, a bit late for breakfast, but maybe her mom was still in there cleaning up.

"Good morning," Lilly said, as she stepped into the kitchen doorway and greeted her mother who sat at the table, nursing a cup of coffee and reading her Bible. She looked just like the mom Lilly had always known. *Maybe I'm just imagining there's a problem. Everyone gets a bit forgetful as they get older. And Dad hasn't made her life easy since the accident.*

Mom lifted her head slowly, as if unsure she'd heard something. Her soft brown eyes registered recognition, awareness now evident on her face. "Lilly!" she cried, jumping up and knocking over her chair. "You came!"

They moved toward one another and embraced, until Lilly pulled back and looked at her mother, who was slightly shorter than she. "Of course I did. Didn't Dad tell you?"

Rachel frowned, her excited eyes fading to confusion. "Tell me what? That you were coming?" She shook her head. "He certainly did not. Besides, how would he know if I didn't?"

The overnight bag slung over Lilly's shoulder seemed to catch her mother's eye. A smile spread across her face. "You're staying?"

Lilly nodded. "Just until Sunday evening. I have to teach next week."

Once again, her mother looked confused. But before either could speak, they heard the rattle of her father's walker. Lilly turned as he entered the room.

"I thought I heard you," he said. "I was watching TV."

Lilly nodded. She had assumed as much. "I just got here. I'm going to go put everything in my room, and then we can all sit down and have a nice visit."

Her father looked less than thrilled at the prospect, but her mother laid her hand on Lilly's forearm. "That

would be wonderful! You can tell us all about college."
She paused. "And you can tell us why they let you come
home before the holidays. Meanwhile, I'll make a fresh
pot of coffee. Are you hungry?"

"Oh no, Mom, not yet. I ate something on the way. I
can wait for lunch."

"Are you sure?"

She smiled. "Yes. I'm sure. Just some coffee would be
fine."

Lilly made her way down the familiar hallway to the
room where she'd slept throughout her entire childhood.
Right now she needed familiarity, as everything else in
her life seemed to be changing at breakneck speed.

Chapter 8

Lilly twisted the strap of her oversized leather purse on her lap. Though she'd attended this church as a child, she'd stopped coming in her mid-teens. Her father had attended a couple of times a year, but her mother rarely missed a Sunday service. Not forced to accompany her mother, Lilly scarcely set foot in a church since.

Yet here I am, waiting to talk to a man I don't really know about something I don't understand. What made me think this was a good idea?

She glanced at her watch. Ten-thirty-five. He was already five minutes late. She'd give him five more—ten, tops—and then she was out of there.

Lilly glanced at the receptionist who'd greeted her warmly when she arrived fifteen minutes earlier. "Pastor Dave shouldn't be long," she'd said after pressing the button on the phone to announce his appointment had arrived.

I wonder what she means by long.

The woman with close-cropped red hair, whose age Lilly imagined was only slightly older than her own, looked up as if she could hear Lilly's thoughts. "He just hung up the phone, so he should be out any minute."

Lilly nodded. *Something tells me this is going to be a big waste of time. I should go.*

She grabbed her purse and was about to stand when the door to the inner office opened, and the man she vaguely remembered meeting at an event a few years earlier smiled at her. "Lilly, I'm sorry I kept you waiting. It's good to see you again. Please, come on in."

Lilly walked toward him, forcing a smile she imagined appeared as wooden as her steps felt. When he ushered her inside, she took a deep breath and followed up on his invitation to have a seat in front of his desk.

"Can I get you some coffee? There's nearly always a pot brewed in the main office."

Lilly shook her head. "No, thank you. Actually, your receptionist offered me some, but I've already reached my limit for the day."

Pastor Dave smiled. "I know what you mean. I drink more than I should." He took a seat behind his desk. "Would it be all right if I open this meeting in prayer? That's my normal practice."

Prayer? So long as all she had to do was close her eyes until he was finished, she imagined a prayer would be all right. She nodded and bowed her head.

"Heavenly Father," the pastor began, "we welcome your presence here, and we ask for wisdom. Guide us as Lilly and I speak to one another, and bless this time together. In your precious name, amen."

Short and sweet. Thank goodness! Lilly opened her eyes and raised her head. The pastor was still smiling. She reinstalled the wooden smile on her face and waited. Should she say something to get the meeting started?

Before she could, Pastor Dave spoke. "It's been quite a while. A Mother's Day event a few years ago, if I remember correctly."

"Yes. I believe you're right." Was he implying she should have been back? "I live several hours from here, so I can't come often."

"Of course. We wouldn't expect you to, but you're always welcome."

Lilly was at a loss for what to say next.

"So, I imagine you're visiting your parents while you're here."

Lilly caught herself before she nodded yet again. She didn't want to look like a bobble-head doll. "Yes. I was here for a few days last week and then I came back last night. I'm working as a substitute teacher, so I have to plan my visits."

This time the pastor nodded. "I remember your mom mentioning that several years ago. She also said something about you doing some freelance writing."

She nodded before she could stop herself, and she felt her cheeks flush. "The writing is really my passion, but I don't make enough to live on. So, I sub at the schools for now. I don't get any financial help from Jacob—" Her cheeks heated, probably a bright red by now. Why had she mentioned her marital situation? It had absolutely nothing to do with the reason for her visit.

Pastor Dave's smile faded, and he leaned forward on his desk, his hands clasped in front of him. "Your mother mentioned something about a divorce—some months ago, I believe. I'm sorry. I know how difficult divorce can be."

Did he really? Somehow she doubted he knew such a difficulty firsthand. She took a deep breath, determined to get back on topic. "It's about Mom. I need to talk to you about her strange behavior. Even my dad has noticed the changes. I thought maybe you had too, and that you might have an idea what's going on with her."

There. She'd stated her concern. She would wait to see his reaction before going any further.

A flicker of understanding softened his dark eyes. "I really haven't seen her much lately, and I feel bad I haven't checked on her more often. She told me she was busy taking care of your dad after the accident, so I didn't really follow through." He shook his head. "That's no excuse. Anyway, I did see her on Sunday. As I told you on the phone, she showed up just after the service ended. I thought that was odd, particularly since we changed the service time quite a while ago, so it's not like she hasn't been here since." He paused before continuing. "Of course, as I said, I knew she was spending more time caring for your dad; and I assumed that was why she hadn't been here lately. Has his condition worsened?"

Lilly swallowed. "Not really. As far as I know, he's about the same, though I sometimes think he could do more if he tried. I'm not even sure he needs the walker. He hasn't been open to discussing any medical issues with me, so I don't ask." She took a deep breath. "To be honest, he doesn't discuss much of anything with me, or Mom, for that matter. He's only recently made an effort to talk with me much at all—mostly about Mom and her—her forgetfulness." She bowed her head and realized she was once again twisting the strap on her purse. She let go and looked back up at the pastor.

"That's ... really why I'm here. Mom seems to forget so many things these days—not just normal things, once in a while, but all sorts of things. For instance, she somehow believes I'm still in college back east. She can't grasp the fact I've been out of college for years now, and I've been married for several of those years. Since she doesn't seem to remember I'm out of college, I haven't even bothered to remind her I'm divorced. Well, almost."

The final words seemed to prick her heart like a pin, and she felt herself deflating. The pastor was going to have to take the initiative from here. She'd said all she could.

After a moment, Pastor Dave said, "I'm sorry to hear about the divorce, Lilly. I know that's not what you came to discuss, so I'll stick to the subject. I must admit, had you come and said these things to me as recently as last week, before I saw your mom after service, I would have been a lot more surprised. What you've said seems to line up with what I saw on Sunday." He cleared his throat. "And you say your dad seems concerned too."

Lilly nodded again, no longer thinking about her bobbing head. "Yes. And for him to mention Mom's forgetfulness means she must be pretty bad." She concentrated on breathing normally and evenly. The last thing she needed was to hyperventilate—or worse yet, start crying.

The pastor leaned back in his chair, tenting his fingers in front of him. "It's been about three years since the accident, right?"

Another nod. "Yes."

"If I remember correctly, your mother was driving. Did she normally drive the car when your father went with her?"

Lilly shook her head. "No. Not really. Dad almost always drove. Mom said for some reason, she really wanted to drive that day. Dad argued, but she insisted. So, of course, when they ended up in an accident, she blamed herself. Especially since Dad was hurt and she wasn't."

Pastor Dave sat forward again. "I understand the accident wasn't her fault. The other driver ran the red light and plowed into them. Even the police report confirmed what happened, right?"

Lilly sighed. "Right. The other driver wasn't hurt either. And Mom said Dad wouldn't have been hurt if she'd just let him drive, like he wanted to." Lilly shook her head. "I suppose she might have been hurt instead, since she would've been the one in the passenger seat. I've tried to talk sense to her about that, but my words just hit a brick wall."

He pressed his lips together, his expression grim. "Self-imposed guilt is a tough thing to get past. Still, I know your mother has a relationship with the Lord—maybe not as close these days as it once was, but there, nonetheless." He shook his head. "I can't help but think the accident and its aftermath have affected her in some deeply negative way."

"You think that's why she's getting so forgetful?"

He shrugged and took a deep breath. "I really don't know, Lilly. And since the accident was three years ago and she's only started exhibiting this behavior recently, something else might be the cause."

"What else?" she asked, steeling herself to speak the words haunting her thoughts for the past week. "Maybe ... dementia? Alzheimer's?"

For a moment, neither spoke. Then the pastor sighed. "Possibly. Of course, there's no way of knowing for sure, based only on something you and your dad have noticed recently. How old is your mom?"

"Sixty-seven. She'll be sixty-eight in a few months."

"I see. She's younger than most people I've known with Alzheimer's, but then I'm hardly an expert on the subject. We have a couple of elderly parishioners who have been diagnosed with dementia. Both now live with their grown children and their families, so I don't see them much anymore. I also know of one lady in our congregation whose mother has the disease, but she's in a home for people with similar situations. I understand it's a good place but quite expensive. I'm sure that's why most seniors with Alzheimer's live with family if possible." He hesitated. "Forgive me if I'm getting ahead of myself here. We have no idea if your mom even has Alzheimer's, and I imagine there's no way to really know unless she sees a doctor for a diagnosis." He frowned. "Do you think she'd be open to that?"

Lilly shook her head. "I have no idea. All of this has just suddenly come out of nowhere, and I feel like my head is reeling with what all this may mean." Unbidden tears teased her eyes, but she blinked them away. "What should I do, Pastor? How do I even begin to deal with this?"

Pastor Dave rose from his chair and came around to her side of the desk, seating himself in the empty chair next to Lilly. He reached over and took one of her hands in his. "I will admit ... I have no idea," he said softly. "But

I know the one who does. Let's pray again."

This time Lilly didn't mind. She closed her eyes and bowed her head, waiting for some sort of answer. Deep down, though, she didn't really expect one.

Rachel was grateful for the peaceful day. Pete hadn't growled at her—much— and even seemed to be concerned about her to some degree. *I wonder why. He hasn't shown concern for me in quite a while. Not since ...*

She sighed. *Not since the accident. Of course. When everything changed ....*

She shook her head, as she sat at the kitchen table, sipping a cup of herbal tea and reflecting on the day. She continued to grasp at the fragile hope they would one day move past the events of that awful time when, for a reason she couldn't even remember, she'd insisted on driving home from ...

Rachel couldn't remember the details either. She was only sure she'd refused to let Pete drive, and he had been the one injured on their ride home. No doubt she deserved any guilt she felt, not to mention the regrets. She knew God could forgive her; maybe Pete would forgive her one day. But could she ever forgive herself?

She took another sip of tea, just as Lilly walked into the kitchen. "Here you are," she said. "I've been sitting with Dad in the TV room and thought you might come join us."

Rachel had nearly forgotten Lilly was here. When had she arrived, and how long would she stay? Before she posed the question, she realized she'd probably already asked, maybe more than once, something she often did these days.

Rachel shook her head. Her forgetfulness was a puzzle, but now wasn't the time to try to arrange the pieces. "I'm so glad you're here," she said, smiling at her daughter.

Lilly returned the smile and sat down beside her mother. "So am I. And it seems I came at exactly the right time. The weather has turned out to be gorgeous, but I know it won't last long."

One of the few things she seemed to be certain of lately was that the beautiful warm days they sometimes enjoyed in the Pacific Northwest were the exception. Rain and cold temperatures were certain to come—sooner rather than later—possibly before the start of the next day.

A snapshot of Wildflower Community Church popped into her mind, and she set her mug down with a *thunk*. "What day is it? Do you know?"

Lilly's perfectly shaped eyebrows lifted, and once again Rachel marveled at her daughter's natural beauty. She scarcely wore any makeup, but she didn't need to. Her nearly perfect complexion complemented her short but stylish reddish-gold hair. *Looks like mine when I was young. Why in the world hasn't some smart young man snatched her up by now? Though she should finish college first.*

"It's Wednesday," Lilly answered. "Why?"

"I thought it might be." Rachel glanced at her watch, then back at her daughter. "If we hurry, we can make midweek service. Wouldn't that be nice?"

A flash of misgiving moved across Lilly's face. "I ... I hadn't planned on going, Mom. I'm sorry, but I'd rather not. And from what I hear, you haven't been going much either."

Rachel's heart sank for a moment. Then she squared her shoulders and took a deep breath. "You're right. And I understand, sweetheart. It was just an idea."

Lilly pushed her chair back and stood up. "Why don't we watch TV with Dad? Doesn't that sound like a good idea?"

Rachel forced a smile. "Sure. You go on. I'll join you later."

When Lilly was gone, Rachel went to her room and picked up her purse and Bible. She might have to go alone, but she was determined to go to church. *I think that's what's been wrong with me. I haven't been going to church like I used to, and I miss the worship and fellowship. Tonight is a good time to reverse that trend, and I know church will do me good.*

She made her way down the hall and through the kitchen and laundry room to the garage door, picking up her keys on the way. She climbed into the car and started the engine, hit the garage door button, and waited while it slid up. Then she backed out into the driveway as she looked behind her.

Almost immediately, she sucked in her breath, as her heart jackhammered inside her. *Where's the street? I can't see it. It's so dark! How will I ever make it to the church?*

Grasping the steering wheel, she laid her head on her hands and cried.

"Where's your mother? Is she still sitting in the kitchen? She does that a lot these days, especially after a meal."

Lilly, who occupied the rocker next to her dad's recliner, looked at her father and frowned. Where was her mother anyway? Hadn't she said she'd come and join them in the TV room? That was nearly thirty minutes ago. Where was she, indeed?

"I'll go check on her." Lilly rose from her chair and returned to the kitchen, expecting to see her mother in the same spot she'd been earlier, but the kitchen was empty.

A sense of unease stirred in the pit of her stomach and moved upward to clutch her chest. *Stop overreacting,* she told herself. *Mom's probably in her room.*

Trying not to show her concern, Lilly hurried down the hall and past the TV room and then opened the door to her parents' dark bedroom. She flipped on the light and realized the room was empty, as was the chair where her mother kept her purse. Unease kicked Lilly into overdrive.

This time, as she passed the TV room, she heard her father call out, "Did you find her?" She ignored him and headed through the kitchen and laundry room toward the garage. She hadn't heard the garage door open, but the TV might have drowned out the noise. "Please, God, let her be all right," she prayed softly, berating herself for praying to a deity she wasn't even sure existed.

Her worst fears washed over her in waves when she saw the garage door open and the inside parking space empty. Then she realized the garage was illuminated by headlights coming from the driveway. As the pieces fell into place, she hurried to her mother's car, which idled but didn't move, and tried to open the driver's door. When Lilly realized it was locked, she rapped on the window, grateful to see her mother sitting there with her head leaning on the steering wheel. At least Mom hadn't driven away.

"Mom! Mom, it's me, Lilly. Open the door."

Slowly, her mother raised her head and turned to look out the window. Lilly could tell she'd been crying.

"Open the door, Mom," Lilly tried to keep the panic from her voice. "Please, Mom. Unlock the door."

As if in slow motion, Mom's face registered recognition. She nodded, then hit the door locks. When Lilly realized her mother wasn't going to turn off the engine and get out, she hurried to the passenger side and climbed in beside her mother.

"Where are you going, Mom?" Lilly reached across the seat and took her mom's right hand in hers. "It's late, Mom. And dark. You shouldn't be going anywhere this late."

"I ..." Mom seemed unable to concentrate for a moment. At last she said, "It's Wednesday night, and I wanted to go to church. I *need* to go to church, Lilly."

Lilly willed back the tears filling her eyes. "I'm sorry, Mom. I didn't realize how badly you wanted to go." She took a deep breath. "How about this? I'm not going home until Sunday afternoon anyway, so maybe you and I can go to church together on Sunday morning. What do you think?"

Mom hesitated. "I suppose so. Will we be home in time for you to catch your plane and get back to college for your Monday classes?"

Lilly's heart twisted. She resisted the urge to explain once again that she'd been out of college a long time and had driven, not flown, to her parents' home. Better to skip the details and simply address the primary issue. "Yes, Mom. We'll be back in plenty of time. Let's plan on going. We'll even eat out afterward."

Mom's smile reached to her brown eyes. "I'd like that," she said. "Can we go to that wonderful sandwich shop I like so well?"

Lilly smiled in return. "We can go anywhere you want, Mom. Your choice. But for now, let's park the car in the garage and go back into the house. All right?"

Mom put the car in drive, and while Lilly held her breath, pulled safely into the familiar parking spot.

Chapter 9

Sunday arrived far too quickly, as far as Rachel was concerned. The last couple of days had seemed clearer than usual, perhaps because Lilly was home to help keep things running smoothly.

Rachel sighed, as she sat in the passenger seat of Lilly's car, wondering yet again why her daughter had driven so far, rather than flying. At least she knew they were heading for church together, and she was pleased. She'd invited Pete to join them. He declined, just as she knew he would. *At least Lilly is going with me today.* Rachel turned to smile at her lovely daughter, who sat with eyes straight ahead, looking out the windshield.

The same familiar thoughts rolled through Rachel's mind, but they didn't seem repetitive at all. *Lilly is so beautiful. Smart too. She's going to make somebody a great wife and mother someday—but not until she's finished college, of course. I just wish she weren't so far away, so she could come home more often.*

Lilly turned into the church driveway and parked in the first vacant space she saw. The weather was cooler today, with quite a bit of cloud cover. Rachel hadn't heard any immediate predictions of rain but was glad she always kept an umbrella in the trunk in case the clouds decided to unleash—a habit Pete had instilled in her when they were first married—a comforting habit even after all these years.

Settling into a pew five rows from the front, Rachel's heart felt suddenly full. She laid her hand on top of Lilly's, which rested on her lap, clasping a church bulletin. Lilly flashed her mother a smile, and Rachel thought she hadn't felt this happy since—since ... she couldn't remember when.

"This means so much to me," she whispered. "Thank you for coming."

Rachel noticed her daughter's eyes tear up, though she knew the strong-willed young woman would never allow them to spill over in public. Lilly smiled, then gently pulled her hand away and began to peruse the bulletin.

From the corner of her eye, Rachel watched her daughter throughout the service, pleased Lilly joined in the singing and seemingly attentive during Pastor Dave's sermon. *She'll probably retain more of it than I will. As hard as I try, I just don't seem to remember things the way I used to.* Rachel frowned. Did she forget things all the time? She wasn't sure.

The fearful, confused feelings she often felt these days threatened to sweep over her, but she steeled herself against them. She was determined not to let anything steal the joy she felt at sitting next to her daughter in church. Lilly had promised to go out to eat after the service, and Rachel wanted nothing more than for the two of them to have a pleasant time before Lilly returned to school.

I'll be so glad when she graduates. This time, Rachel realized she repeated these particular thoughts many times throughout the day. *I just pray she finds a job closer to home so we can spend more time together.*

They'd just returned to Lilly's car when she smiled and asked, "So, Mom, did you decide where you want to go for lunch?"

Rachel grinned. "There's a great little Italian place, just down the street. Can we go there?"

Lilly's smile faded slightly. "Sure. So you don't want to go to the sandwich place you mentioned the other night?"

Rachel pursed her lips, trying to remember what sandwich shop her daughter might be talking about. Coming up empty, she shook her head. "I'm sorry, honey. I don't know about any sandwich shops around here. Is that what you want for lunch?"

Lilly patted Rachel's hand. "Italian sounds perfect, Mom. But let's remember to order something to go for Dad. You know how he gets when he has to fix his own lunch."

So true. There were a lot of things Rachel couldn't remember these days, but how Pete got when he was hungry and thought he'd been deserted was not one of them.

✵❋✿✧

Pete was amazed at how much better his wife had seemed since their daughter left. He had thought the opposite would be true, but he wasn't about to stir things up by asking Rachel.

His breakfast was even cooked right—eggs over easy, bacon crisp, toast with strawberry jam, no butter. Best of all, the coffee was hot and strong, the way he liked it.

"Nice breakfast," he commented, grabbing another half-slice of toast. "Best in a while."

Rachel lifted her head, a smile spreading across her face, as her eyes lit up. "Thank you, Pete. I've really been trying."

He gave a curt nod. "I can tell." He chomped down on his toast, the conversation over as far as he was concerned.

Apparently Rachel didn't feel the same way, as she laid her hand on his forearm and said, "I just want us to be a family again. That's all."

Pete frowned. What was she talking about? They'd been a family for nearly forty-five years. What was different now? Unsure of how to respond to her comment, he grunted and went on eating.

"I was wondering ..."

Now what? He shifted his gaze from his plate to his wife.

"With Lilly back at school and the two of us having some spare time, why don't we go out and do something special today?" Her glance darted toward the window and back. "The sun's out, but it's supposed to start raining again tomorrow. Let's take advantage of the good weather and go do something together—like we used to."

Tension seeped into his shoulders, and his neck stiffened. She'd driven him to two doctor's appointments earlier this month, plus Lilly had stocked them up on groceries and picked up their prescriptions at the pharmacy before she left. Where else did they need to go? He wasn't anxious to get back into the car with his forgetful wife unless it was a real emergency.

He sighed. He'd known Rachel long enough to realize she wouldn't leave him alone about this until he gave her a straight answer. "So what do you have in mind? You don't need anything from the store already, do you?"

The light he'd seen in her eyes faded quickly. As usual, he'd said the wrong thing. He never seemed to know how to approach her these days.

"I ... I hoped maybe we could go somewhere else—not the doctor or the grocery store."

Pete laid his fork across his plate. "Such as?"

She shrugged, beginning to twist her wedding ring, something Pete had noticed she did a lot lately, particularly when she seemed nervous. "Oh, I don't know," she said, hesitation in her voice. "A movie, maybe? Or just a nice drive over to the coast to have lunch somewhere?"

"Do you know how long a drive that is, over and back?" He shook his head. "No, Rachel. I'm sorry, but no. The last time I let you drive me even half that distance ... well, you know what happened. You don't think I'm going to risk something like that again, do you? Some trips close to home are one thing—a necessity, I suppose since I can't drive anymore. But anything else? Not a chance."

She glanced toward his walker and back. Tears brimmed in her brown eyes, something that would have melted his heart at one point in their marriage. Now, he steeled himself against her tears. "Besides," he added, inserting a stern note into his voice to convince her the discussion was closed, "we can't afford a trip. You know how tight things are now that neither of us can work anymore. We're on a fixed income, remember? That means nothing extra—necessities only."

A tear spilled down her cheek, but he hardened himself and returned to his meal. Who knew when she'd make him another one quite so good? He imagined she'd soon slip back into her usual confused state.

The breakfast dishes had been washed and the kitchen cleaned up. Pete had retired to his usual seat in the TV room, and Rachel had retreated to the guest room, which was quickly becoming her safe place. Her heart ached as she recalled the conversation at breakfast. She'd been so hopeful, especially since her mind had seemed so much clearer lately. Maybe this forgetfulness was just a virus or something, and now she was back to normal.

In her heart, she knew this wasn't true, but she was already too sad to let herself think otherwise. She stroked the familiar quilt covering the bed where she sat. Oh, the memories this quilt evoked—her childhood, her parents, the happy times …

"I miss you, Mama," she whispered. "Daddy, too, of course, but you, Mama, especially. I keep telling myself to do the next thing, the way you taught me. But sometimes I just don't know what the next thing is. Oh, Mama, you were always there for me, to help me sort things out, to ease the hurts and celebrate the joys. How I wish you were here now. I really need you, Mama. I need to talk to you."

You can talk to me.

The voice seemed to come out of nowhere, yet its familiarity and comfort were immediate. Slipping to her knees beside the bed, Rachel's heart raced. She hadn't heard God's voice in so long, or at least as long as she could remember. Did she dare hope he wished to speak to her again?

I am here, daughter, waiting for you. You can come and talk to me anytime.

She nodded, a lump forming in her throat. "Yes," she managed to whisper. "I know. Why can't I remember to talk to you more often?"

Your heart cries out to me many times during the day— deep calling to deep—and I always answer.

Tears spilled over onto her cheeks. She folded her hands and laid them on the bed as she cried and silently prayed. *What's wrong with me, Lord? Why can't I remember things? There are days when my memory's not so bad, like right now. But other times ... Oh, Father, I am so scared!*

A butterfly-light touch, seeming to stroke her hair, sent a thrill of joy racing through her. "You're truly here, aren't You, Lord?" she whispered. "Right here with me."

She could almost see him smile. *I am always with you, daughter. I promised never to leave you, and I always keep my promises.*

Rachel took a deep breath and let it out in a shudder. *But I feel as if I'm losing my mind.* She tried to swallow the lump in her throat, as she listened for the answer. She didn't have long to wait.

You needn't worry. Just know when you are too weak to walk, I am carrying you. Nothing will stop my purposes for your life. When you breathe your last on this earth, you will be with me forever. You gave your heart to me when you were just a child, daughter. You have been mine from that day forward. Nothing can change that.

As she relaxed under the Father's touch and meditated on his words, she felt a warmth flow over her heart. Somehow she knew then even if her mind wasn't whole, her heart would be.

Chapter 10

Lilly ended her phone conversation with Pastor Dave and leaned back in her favorite recliner. Before calling him, she'd checked in with her parents, as she'd done at least once daily since returning home. Until today, her mother had been the one to answer the phone; this time her dad answered. Not a good sign.

"How's everything going, Dad?"

"Better—until today."

Her heartrate kicked up a notch. "What do you mean?"

"I told you. She was doing okay after you left. I was surprised because I thought she'd be worse—you know, with you gone and all. She still thought you were away at college but also thought you'd be coming for the holidays soon, and that seemed to make her happy. She was even doing a good job in the kitchen again. But now ..."

"Now what?" she asked, nearly holding her breath for the answer.

"Now she's back to the way she was before—maybe even worse. I try to talk sense into her, but it doesn't do any good. Sometimes she looks at me like she doesn't know who I am. Truth is, I'm the one who doesn't know my wife these days."

Lilly felt as if her heart had plummeted to her feet. She had so hoped her suspicions were wrong, and her mom was pulling out of whatever slump she'd been in. Now she knew that wasn't the case ... nor did it seem it would ever be.

That thought convinced her to call Pastor Dave. "I thought maybe she was doing better," she told him. "She was a bit confused when I was there, but we had a great visit and a lot of fun together—almost like we used to. Even after I left, Dad said she was doing okay." She sighed. "But I just talked to him, and he says she's at least as bad as before. I'm afraid she has Alzheimer's. It seems obvious now, don't you think?"

The pastor paused for a moment before answering. Was he thinking or praying? "It's too soon to give up hope," he said at last. "She hasn't even seen a doctor about this yet, has she?"

Lilly shook her head, a reflex since he couldn't see her. "No. When I was there, I asked her when she'd last seen the doctor. She said she hadn't been to see him in several weeks. When I asked her what the doctor said, she started telling me about my dad's situation. Apparently, the appointment had been for him not her. So I asked her again when she'd seen the doctor for herself. She couldn't remember. I asked Dad, but he said he had no idea. Obviously, it's been a while—too long, I imagine."

"I'm so sorry," Pastor Dave said. "I can't imagine how hard this is on you, but things may not be as bad as you think. I don't know where you are in your relationship with the Lord, but your mother has walked with him since she was a child. She belongs to him, and he loves her deeply. None of this has caught him by surprise, Lilly."

Her jaws clenched, and she wanted to spit resentment. At last she gave in and spewed her thoughts aloud. "Really, Pastor? Because if my mother's condition didn't catch the Lord by surprise, then he knew this would happen. And if she supposedly belongs to and is loved by him, why would he let something like this happen to her?"

Again, the pastor paused before responding. "I understand your feelings, Lilly. I truly do. That's probably the most-asked question I hear as a pastor. Why would a good and loving God let bad things happen? I may not have a specific answer for your mom's situation. However, in general, what may seem bad to us can very well turn around and end up being good—whether we see the good or not. Even in the Bible, Joseph, who was sold into slavery by his own brothers, later told them what they'd meant for evil God had meant for good. God always intends for our good, even though we might not understand the why. This is faith, Lilly. Your mother has faith, and I pray your dad will too someday. But what about you? Do you have faith? If so, is your faith based on how many blessings God pours out on us, or are your beliefs based on his Word and his goodness?"

Lilly couldn't give a ready answer. When Pastor Dave spoke again, asking if he could pray with her, she answered as politely as possible, "Not right now. Later, if you'd like ... when I'm not there ... or when I'm not feeling so discouraged and angry. I'm sorry, but that's just what I'm feeling right now."

Pastor Dave was gracious, telling her he understood and respected her feelings promising to pray for her after he hung up—and daily after that.

She disconnected, shook her head, and mentally rehashed the conversation. How could she stay mad at someone like Pastor Dave? He was kind and understanding, and she knew he wanted only the best for her and her family.

"So maybe it's not the pastor I'm mad at," she said aloud. "Maybe it's you, God." She grabbed the remote from the table by her phone. "Yep," she said, clicking on the TV, determined to lose herself in a movie. "I am most certainly mad at you, God—if you even exist. If unbelief makes me a horrible person, then I guess that's who I am. But I prayed, God. I prayed long and hard for a baby, but you didn't answer. And then, you took away my husband. Couldn't you at least let me have a little peace before springing all this about my mom on me?"

Hot tears bit her eyes. Once again, she refused to let them flow. She clicked through the channels until she saw something promising. "Signing off now, God," she said. "I'll let you know if anything changes."

Another weekend had rolled around, and Lilly found herself once again nearing her hometown. She rose long before daylight and drove the not-quite four hours straight through. When she pulled into town, she wanted nothing more than to get to her parents' home, excuse herself, go to her old room, and take a nap. First, she must keep her appointment with Pastor Dave. She parked her car but sat for a few minutes, gathering courage.

She thought of the call she'd received yesterday from Kelly, Pastor Dave's assistant requesting Lilly set up an appointment with the pastor. Lilly was going to visit her parents anyway and had agreed to meet with Pastor Dave at the church at noon on Saturday.

When she'd hung up, she tried to ignore the tightness in her chest. What did the pastor want to talk about? Did he know something she didn't? Had the situation with her mother gotten worse? Surely, if so, her dad would have let her know. Wouldn't he?

And so she'd called and talked briefly to each of her parents. Neither mentioned anything unusual, so Lilly did her best to put her fears to rest. After all, she would find out more the next day. However, the waiting only seemed to build upon her mounting concerns as she waited in front of Wildflower Community Church.

She gathered courage and, in a matter of minutes, was sitting across the desk from the pastor, encouraged by his welcoming smile. Maybe he didn't have bad news for her after all.

"Coffee?" he asked.

She blinked. Had he said something?

He held up his cup. "I just made fresh coffee. Would you like some?"

"Oh, no, thank you. I ..." Her hands felt cold, so why not wrap them around a warm cup? Besides, she was feeling a bit sleepy after getting up so early and driving non-stop. "Actually, yes. I would like some. Thank you."

He got up and walked to a small table just outside his office door, which he'd left open since no one was in the outer office. "Cream and sugar?"

"Black, please."

Moments later she was clutching the cup in her hands, anxious to know why he wanted to speak with her. Should she say something, or should she wait for him to initiate conversation?

He answered her question for her, as he leaned forward, his forearms resting on his desk and his fingers interlaced in front of him. "Have you kept in touch with your parents since we last spoke?"

She took a sip of coffee and nodded. "Yes. I try to call at least once a day. Dad answers most of the time now, which is a real change for him. Since the ... accident, he hasn't exactly been a master communicator." She smiled nervously and was relieved when Pastor Dave returned her smile. Encouraged to go on, she said, "Dad said Mom was doing better for a few days but seems to have slipped away again." She sighed. "I always ask to talk to Mom. She seems happy to hear from me, but she also seems to think I'm still in my early twenties and at college." Lilly shook her head. "I don't think she remembers I've been married." She couldn't say anything more and waited for the pastor to speak.

Pastor Dave sighed. "I called her in the middle of the week. When your dad answered, I thought I'd talk to him first." He paused. "He cut me off too fast, though, and put your mom on. So I talked to her instead. That was a couple of days ago, and she obviously knew who I was. But I got the distinct impression her mind was somewhere else, possibly in the past."

Lilly clasped her hands together. So she wasn't the only one who felt Mom had slipped back a few years. Lilly had learned enough about Alzheimer's to know this sort of memory loss was a common symptom, but surely there could be other explanations.

She looked into Pastor Dave's dark eyes, hoping to find some sort of answer there. Why had he requested this appointment? Surely there was a specific reason.

"I know you're wondering why I had Kelly call you to set up an appointment. I'm glad you decided to come to the church rather than talking on the phone. I just wish I had some encouraging news for you, something to convince you—both of us, actually—your mother doesn't have some form of dementia." He dropped his head briefly, seeming to study his folded hands, then said, "Truthfully, Lilly, I can't imagine anything else. I think we have to face the fact she may very well be in the early stages of Alzheimer's, though I pray I'm wrong. There's no way for us to know for sure without getting her to see a doctor. We've touched on this before. Are you open to encouraging her to see her doctor now? And if so, how do you think she'll respond?"

Lilly took a deep breath. "I honestly have no idea. I've been thinking the same thing, and I'm fine with trying to convince her to see a doctor. But what if she refuses? I don't think she's been to the doctor for herself in years. Since the accident, no doubt. The only doctor visits she's been to since then are for Dad. He can't drive anymore, as I'm sure you know, so ..."

Getting her mother to agree to see a doctor would be no easy task since she didn't believe anything was wrong with her. How should the subject be broached?

The pastor cleared his throat. "Speaking of your dad, I've been wondering if he would be open to talking with me. I think getting his perspective would be helpful. But he hasn't been to church in ages, and even then he only came occasionally—mostly to please your mom, I think. When I'd call, he seemed to be in a hurry to pass the phone off to your mother. What do you think, Lilly? I feel like I should at least try to talk to him, don't you agree? Of course, I'd like to talk to your mom, too, but if I go by the house to see her, I need to let your dad know ahead of time why I'm coming."

His reasoning made perfect sense. If the pastor stopped by to see her mom without her dad knowing why, he might think they were talking about him. She sighed again. How had things gotten to the point she had to be careful what she said to her own parents? They had all been so close once—they could and did talk about anything. Now she was guarded in what she said to her mother for fear of confusing her more than she already was. And talking to her dad was only slightly better these last few weeks—no doubt because he'd been forced to admit his wife wasn't behaving normally.

"Maybe you should approach him first. I'll mention you'd like to talk with him before talking with Mom. I'll even offer to be there if that makes him more comfortable." She shrugged. "Honestly, I have no idea how he'll respond."

Pastor Dave nodded. "All right. I'll wait until I hear from you. Before I had Kelly call you yesterday, I thought we should explore options, like support groups and in-house care. But maybe it's still too early. The first thing is to get your mom to a doctor. Meanwhile ..."

He came around to the front of his desk and sat down in the chair next to hers, much as he had the last time she was there. She knew exactly what he was going to say before he spoke.

"Meanwhile, let's pray, shall we? You and I don't know what's going on with your mom, but God does. And we really need his guidance in sorting all this out."

She closed her eyes, ignoring the hint of tears threatening so often these days. Then she bowed her head, her heart heavy, even as she dared to hope there was some explanation for her mother's behavior other than dementia.

Lilly had mixed emotions as she pulled into her parents' driveway. She looked forward to seeing them, as she always did, but dreaded the conversation she knew she must initiate. How would her mother react to the suggestion she see a doctor—for herself, not for her husband?

Maybe I can convince her if I offer to rearrange my schedule so I can go with her to the appointment.

She let herself in and immediately realized her parents weren't up yet. Heading straight down the hallway, she set her things in her old room and then returned to the kitchen to make coffee. The cup she'd had with Pastor Dave was scarcely enough, particularly with what she had on her agenda for today.

The rich dark liquid had just begun to brew and send its tantalizing aroma drifting out of the kitchen and down the hallway toward the bedrooms when Lilly heard her parents' bedroom door open. In less than a minute, her mother stood in the kitchen doorway, clutching her old blue robe around her middle, her hair sticking up in back. Her brown eyes were wide. With fear? Confusion? Lilly couldn't tell.

"Hi, Mom," she said, smiling as she went to hug her mother and plant a kiss on her cheek. "I'm sorry if I woke you, but I really needed some coffee after such a long drive."

She pulled back and looked down into her mother's face. Her wide eyed glance had given way to a frown.

"What are you doing here?" she asked.

Lilly's heart squeezed. They'd just had this conversation on the phone the previous night, and she'd convinced her mother there would be no problem for her to break away for a short visit.

"I'm here for the weekend," Lilly explained. "Remember? We talked about my coming last night."

Her mother tilted her head to the left, as if she thought the gesture would help her process her daughter's words. "But what about school? It seems you've been missing a lot of classes lately. And how can you afford all these plane tickets?"

Lilly took her mom's hand and led her to the kitchen table. "I'm not missing classes, Mom. My schedule is just fine. And I'm not flying back and forth; I'm driving." She pulled out a chair and indicated to her mother to have a seat. "Let me get you a cup of coffee. I'll have some too. Do you want anything to eat?"

Mom took a seat and shook her head in response to Lilly's offer. "Not yet. Maybe later."

Lilly cancelled her plans to make eggs and toast, though she was hungry and wouldn't mind having something. Perhaps she should wait until both her parents were up and ready for breakfast.

Lilly returned to the table with two steaming mugs and sat next to her mother. She took a welcomed sip, then wrapped her hands around the mug, wondering what to say next. Should she just plunge right into the subject and see how her mother reacted, or should she put out a few feelers first?

She opted for the second action. *Coward that I am.* "So, Mom, what have you been up to since my last visit? Anything interesting going on I don't know about?"

The puzzled look danced across her mother's face again before she shook her head. "Nothing," she mumbled, taking a sip of coffee. "You know how things are around here. Your dad spends most of his day in front of the TV. I join him occasionally, but I really don't enjoy watching television that much."

Lilly nodded. "So what do you do when you're not watching TV with Dad?"

The question seemed to catch her mother off-guard. "I … I don't know. I suppose I cook or do laundry. And I'm nearly certain I do the dishes, and even the vacuuming and ironing occasionally. You know, the usual."

"That's all?"

"Sometimes I …" She sighed. "Sometimes, when the weather's nice, I go and sit in the backyard or on the porch swing out in front. But it's been too cold and wet for that lately. So I go to my retro-room and think about Mama and Daddy." She smiled, her eyes wistful. "It's nice to spend time with them again. I've missed them terribly. Sometimes Mama even talks to me. When she doesn't, I get out the albums and go through them. The pictures make me feel young again—and happy."

Was this her opening? Lilly wasn't sure, but she decided to take a chance. "So when you think of the past, you feel happy. Does this mean you're not happy now?"

Mom set her cup down and leaned back in her seat, her eyes seeming to search for an answer. "I … I don't know," she said at last. "I suppose I'm happy. I mean, there's no reason not to be, right? I just don't know."

Lilly clasped her mother's hand. "Mom, sometimes we feel at loose ends and unclear on things—when we have something physical going on we don't know about. You haven't seen the doctor for yourself in ages. Right?"

Her mother nodded grudgingly. "I suppose," she admitted. "Your dad's the one who needs the doctor, not me. I take him to all his appointments, and I make sure he takes his medicine."

"I know you do," Lilly said, "and that's a very commendable thing. You're a good wife to Dad, and a good caretaker too. But sometimes we have to take care of ourselves so we can take care of others. Do you understand, Mom?"

"Sort of," she said. "Yes. I mean, actually, I do understand what you're saying. I've even thought a couple of times I should go in for a checkup. You're right. It *has* been far too long. Maybe I'll call on Monday and make an appointment."

A good first step, but her mother's resolve could melt away with her other memories. "Tell you what," Lilly said. "I'm going to be here until Monday, so I'll make the appointment for you. Then, if we can't get you in right away, I'll go home and come back in time to take you. What do you think, Mom?" She smiled encouragingly. "Is it a date?"

Rachel shook her head. "No, it's not. I don't want you missing anymore school on my account. You need to get back to classes right away. I can get myself to the doctor."

"Okay. We'll see what happens. But I'm staying over until Monday morning, regardless. I'll make the appointment for you, and we'll take it from there. Okay?"

Mom scowled as if she didn't approve, but she offered no argument. Retrieving her mug of coffee, she took a sip. "It's almost cold. Can you warm it for me?"

"Of course." Lilly took both their cups to the sink. She emptied them and then refilled them with hot coffee.

Before she returned to the table, Mom brightened a little. "I'm hungry," she said. "Would you mind fixing me something to eat, sweetheart?"

Lilly smiled. "Of course I wouldn't mind. I'm hungry too. Why don't you go see if Dad's awake yet? If he is, I'll make something for all of us."

Her mother rose and left the kitchen. Lilly heaved a sigh of relief as she took out the eggs and butter from the refrigerator.

Chapter 11

Lilly had managed to get an appointment for her mother for Thursday morning and convinced her there was no need to return to school before Monday. Lilly thought she could work on her writing assignment in the meantime.

When Thursday rolled around, she asked her father if he'd like to come with them for her mother's appointment. Looking up from the TV screen, he frowned. "Why would I want to do that? She's got you to take her, right? If you find out something I should know, you can tell me when you get back."

Lilly suppressed a sigh. "Sure, Dad. No problem."

When the appointment time came, Lilly and her mother waited in the small exam room, each perched on a small armchair against the wall, not more than a couple of feet from the examination table and the doctor's wheeled stool.

"I'm still not sure why we're here," Mom said, not for the first time that morning. "There's nothing wrong with me. I feel fine."

Lilly laid a hand on her mother's arm. "I know you do, Mom. But you're sixty-seven years old. You need to come for regular check-ups." Lilly smiled. "Humor me, okay? I'll feel better when the doctor confirms you're in good health."

Her mother turned away, seeming to offer silent agreement to her daughter's words, even as she twisted her wedding ring.

Within minutes, the door opened. The middle-aged man in the white coat, who had been her parents' doctor even before the accident, walked in. The blue tag over the pocket of his white coat read, *James Clark, M.D.* His thin hair was combed to the right, and his gray eyes smiled at them.

Dr. Clark glanced at the record on the computer screen, then sat down on the stool, his eyes fixed on his patient as he wheeled the stool closer. "You finally decided to come in and see me." He chuckled. "I was beginning to think you'd forgotten me."

Mom shook her head. "Oh, no, doctor, not at all. Didn't I just see you not too long ago?"

He smiled. "Sure. I've actually seen you several times over the last few years." He leaned forward. "But it was always for your husband. I'm glad you decided to come in for yourself this time. So how have you been feeling? Any specific complaints?"

The doctor's mention of her father clicked a memory in Lilly's mind. She needed to ask her dad about having the pastor come to speak with Mom. Lilly made a mental note to do so as soon as they got home. Meanwhile, she held her breath. How would her mom respond to the doctor's questions?

She shrugged. "No, not really. Sometimes I get lost when I'm out driving, or I forget where I am and what I'm supposed to be doing. Otherwise, I'm fine."

Dr. Clark's eyes flickered toward Lilly, who tried silently to telegraph him to pursue the getting-lost-and-forgetting part. He quickly returned his attention to Mom.

"What do you mean, you get lost?" he asked. "Is it because you're somewhere unfamiliar?"

She shook her head. "I don't think so. Once I was just going to church. Or was I coming home from church?" She paused, as if trying to pull up the answer to her question. "Another time I found myself on the way to the beach, even though I didn't want to go there." She frowned. "I can't remember how I got home, but I think a nice young man helped me."

"I see." Dr. Clark gave a slight smile. "And is there anything else? Other times when you forgot things or felt confused?"

"Lots of times ... I think. I can't remember for sure. But one time I was at the mall, and when I came out, forgot where I left my car. And sometimes I forget what I'm doing at home, so I go to my retro-room—our guest room—and talk to Mama and Daddy to see if they can help. Mama always tells me to 'do the next thing,' but sometimes I can't figure out what that is."

She smiled then, her eyes going soft. "But when it's really bad, and I think I'm going to start crying and never stop—which would really upset Pete—I talk to God, and he always helps me."

"That sounds like a wise plan," the doctor said. "I talk to God when I'm having trouble figuring things out too."

Mom's face lit up. "You do?"

"Absolutely. It's the one place I can go where I know I'll get the right answer."

Mom's shoulders relaxed. Had they turned a corner?

"How long has this been happening?" the doctor asked, his voice gentle, yet probing.

Her mother sighed. "I'm not sure. I forget things ... like time, you know."

"Yes, I do know. And don't worry. We'll figure this out together, all right?"

Mom seemed at ease now, and the feeling passed to Lilly. Yes, this was all going to be okay. Dr. Clark would find out what was really going on with her mother and then he would tell them what to do.

Pete didn't like the look of things. Ever since Lilly had taken Rachel to the doctor, he'd felt left out. True, he'd been invited to go, but why should he? Couldn't Lilly fill him in on anything he might need to know about his wife?

To be fair, he sensed his daughter had been looking for an opportunity to talk with him alone. Unfortunately, each time there had been an opportunity, Rachel showed up, ready to join them wherever they were.

He sighed. Another week had passed, and Saturday had rolled around again. Lilly planned to go home the next day, after taking her mother to church. If he didn't get a chance to talk with Lilly privately before then, he might never find out what the doctor said. The way Rachel's memory was these days, he surely couldn't count on her to tell him.

Sitting in his favorite chair, he picked up the remote and flipped through the channels. There wasn't much on of interest. He supposed he'd have to settle for a college football game until the pro games on Sunday.

"Hey, Dad."

Lilly's voice caught his attention, and he turned to find her standing just a couple feet from him. When had she come in?

He nodded a silent greeting. "Want to watch some football with me?"

A flicker of uncertainty danced through Lilly's brown eyes, and Pete's attention meter kicked into overdrive. Was he going to find out about Rachel's doctor visit ... at last?

"Sit down," he said, indicating the rocking chair beside him. "What's up?"

Lilly sat, then darted a last look in the direction of the hallway. "Mom said she was going to take a nap. I thought this might be a good time for us to talk."

"About?"

"About Mom's doctor visit. About Mom, period."

He sighed. "I figured as much." He waited, watching as Lilly fingered the fringe on the throw pillow where she sat.

"I ... I know you've noticed some changes with Mom lately. You've mentioned them to me on the phone." She paused. When he didn't respond, she went on. "She's become forgetful. So much so sometimes it seems she has no clue what day—or even what year—it is."

Pete waited. He hadn't yet heard anything he didn't already know.

Lilly lowered her eyes for a moment, as if watching herself fiddle with the pillow fringe. Then she raised her head and looked straight at her father. "I sensed something was wrong, something more than a little forgetfulness. And I know you have too."

He took a deep breath, feeling as if he were waiting for the proverbial other shoe to drop.

"I spoke to Pastor Dave about Mom's confusion, and he was concerned too. He said Mom had shown up at church just as everyone else was leaving. She didn't seem to have any idea the service time had changed, and I know it hasn't been that long since she quit attending."

"I had no idea you were in touch with the pastor," Pete said. "Since when?"

Lilly shrugged. "Only recently—since I've truly begun to believe something might be wrong with Mom."

Pete tilted his head, watching his daughter closely as he wondered where she would go next. What other surprises might she have for him?

"Pastor Dave and I discussed the possibility that ... that mom might have some sort of dementia."

Her entire body seemed to tense as she uttered the last word—the word echoing through Pete's mind now.

Dementia? As in Alzheimer's? He shook his head. "No, that can't be right. Sure, your mom forgets things now and then. But who doesn't, especially when we get older, right?"

Lilly sighed. "I hoped this was the only problem, but deep down I knew better. The pastor convinced me to make sure Mom saw a doctor. That's why I took Mom to see Dr. Clark the other day."

"Yeah. I was beginning to wonder if you'd ever tell me what happened. What did the doctor say is wrong with her?"

Lilly hesitated, as she continued twisting the fringe. "He ... he didn't. Not definitely, anyway. I managed to talk with him alone for a few moments when Mom had to go to the bathroom. He too suspects dementia. He says she has many of the classic symptoms."

"But he's not sure," Pete argued. "It could be something else, right?"

Lilly's voice was low. "Not likely."

Pete felt his heart skip a beat, as fear danced through his mind. He shook his head, a futile attempt to rid himself of the negative feelings. "No. I don't believe it. It can't be. Your mom takes care of me. How can she take care of me if she loses her mind?"

Lilly laid a hand on his arm. "The doctor explained there's no strong or clear guidelines for how this problem will progress—if indeed Mom has Alzheimer's. Since she's only recently begun showing signs, it means she doesn't have early-onset Alzheimer's—the kind that can hit as young as sixty and progresses more quickly than in older people." She sighed again, deeply. "I just hope that's the case with Mom. If so, we could still have several good years left with her before ..."

Pete didn't ask her to finish the sentence. He waited to see if his daughter would say anything else.

She took a deep breath and continued. "Dr. Clark wants to schedule a brain-imaging test to help confirm what he already suspects after talking with Mom. I know you can't drive, Dad, so I gave the doctor my number. He'll work with me to set up her appointment, and I'll keep the day clear to take Mom. Like I told you before, you're invited. I think it would actually be a good thing if you came along and showed your support."

Pete sat quietly, trying to sort through all the new information Lilly had just mounted on him. The only thing pounding louder than his heart was his head. "So, do you want to watch some football with me? I think Notre Dame is playing."

Lilly's brown eyes opened wide, and he knew he hadn't scored any points with his only child.

"No, thanks, Dad. Not right now. I think I'll go check on Mom."

✷ ✳ ✧ ✧

Rachel was exhausted, but she couldn't imagine why. What had she done today to wear her out like this? She desperately wanted to sleep, but her mind wouldn't cooperate.

She lay on her back, forcing her eyes to stay closed, though the light from the nearby window bothered her. The day had been gray and dreary, raining off and on. Now, when she wanted to take a nap, the sun chose to shine, however briefly.

I feel like there's so much going on in my life, but I can't figure out what exactly. I know my main responsibility is taking care of Pete, but everything else is blurred. Well, maybe not everything else. I do know Lilly's been here a lot lately. As much as I enjoy having her home, I can't help but wonder if something is wrong at school. How can she possibly take so much time off and not affect her grades?

A soft knock interrupted her thoughts. Most likely Lilly; Pete wouldn't knock.

"Come in, sweetheart. I'm not asleep."

Rachel opened her eyes as Lilly stepped into the room and then approached the bed. Rachel never ceased to marvel at the beautiful young woman Lilly had become.

We waited and prayed for you for so many years. So often I despaired of ever having a child. But there I was, in my early thirties, and suddenly I found myself pregnant.

Lilly stood at the side of the bed, while Rachel scooted toward the middle to make some room. Lilly accepted the silent invitation and sat down. "I thought sure you'd fallen asleep by now." Lilly reached out to take her mother's hand. "You seemed so sleepy earlier."

"I was. I don't know why I can't seem to fall asleep."

Lilly smiled. "Too much on your mind."

How could she explain her concern wasn't so much what was on her mind, rather what her mind couldn't seem to retain.

"I've been talking to Dad," Lilly said. "I told him Dr. Clark wants to schedule some tests for you. I know Dad can't drive you to your appointment, so I asked the doctor to call me with the time and place for the test. I'll rearrange my schedule so I can come back and take you."

Rachel squeezed her daughter's hand. "That's so sweet of you, but ..." She gathered her courage and plunged in, determined to express her concern and get something resolved. "I don't think that's a good idea. You've missed far too much school already. I'm worried all this time off will hurt your grades." She lifted herself up onto her elbows, peering intently at her daughter. "You are far too intelligent and dedicated to let anything get in the way of your education. You worked hard to get that scholarship, and I'm not about to let you ruin your future because of me." She shook her head. "No, Lilly. You do not need to come and take me to my appointment. I'll drive myself or call a cab. And besides ..." She wasn't really about to tell Lilly a lie, wanting to figure out a statement to help set her priorities straight.

"There's nothing wrong with me," Rachel said, finally. "Truly, sweetheart, I'm fine. You need to stop worrying about me and take care of yourself."

Tears glistened in Lilly's eyes as she reached out to pull her mother into her arms. "I knew you'd say that, Mom. But you need to know you are number-one on my priority list. And there's nothing you can say to keep me from coming here to help you, anytime you need it. So get used to my being here."

Rachel sighed. She wasn't going to be able to talk her daughter out of taking her to her appointment or who knew what else, so she might as well just enjoy being with her.

Tears bit her own eyes. Though she tried to blink them back, a few escaped, spilling onto her cheeks. *Thank You, Lord, for such a wonderful daughter.*

Chapter 12

Two weeks had passed since her mother's first doctor appointment, and now Lilly was once again in conference with Pastor Dave. His eyes mirrored the sadness Lilly felt.

"So the doctor confirmed what we suspected," he said.

"Yes. Though he assured me we could still have many years left with Mom. What he couldn't assure me was if Mom would be aware of them." She blinked back tears. "Her condition will get worse. How quickly, no one knows."

The pastor leaned back in his chair and tented his fingers in front of his face. "I know it's not the diagnosis we hoped to hear, but it's the one we sensed it would be. I'm sorry."

Lilly nodded, at a loss for words.

"Have you talked with your dad since receiving the doctor's confirmation?"

She swallowed the lump in her throat. "Yes. He scarcely commented, though I know he heard and understood me." Lilly shook her head. "That seems to be the way he copes with things—or doesn't, as the case may be. You'd think he'd realize he can't make Mom's illness go away by ignoring it."

Pastor Dave sat forward, leaning his elbows on his desk. "He's dependent on her for nearly everything, isn't he?"

"Yes. It didn't used to be that way, but since the accident ..."

"I know. Things changed drastically then." He sighed. "I remember trying to talk to your father years ago, on the few occasions when I saw him at church. At the time, he wasn't open to speaking with me. Do you suppose he might be now? I could go visit your mom and dad both ... separately or together. What do you think? Did you ever get a chance to ask him if he'd be okay with my visiting?"

Lilly shook her head. "No, I'm afraid I didn't. I thought of asking him several times, but there never seemed to be a right time. As far as his being open to talking to you, I honestly don't know. I assume you mean talking to him about what we're going to do about Mom's situation."

Pastor Dave cleared his throat. "Yes. But what I really meant was, do you think he'd be open to talking about the Lord? As far as I can tell, he's never had a personal relationship with God. As I said, he came to church with your mother on special occasions. Since the accident, he hasn't been even once."

Lilly felt her cheeks warm. This topic was getting a little too close for comfort. The pastor most likely knew she'd accepted the Lord as her Savior when she was a child. He no doubt also knew, or at least strongly suspected, she'd done very little in her adult years to maintain or grow that relationship. How could she point a finger at her father when she herself was guilty as charged?

"I really can't say, Pastor. He might. Honestly, I doubt it. And I'm afraid I wouldn't be the one to open that discussion with him."

Pastor Dave paused before answering. "I understand, and I'm not asking you to. I'm simply asking if you think I should try. Do you have any objections?"

She felt her eyes widen. Admitting her own lack of faith was bad enough, but denying her father the chance to receive or cultivate a faith she no longer claimed was something else. "Of course not." She cleared her throat. "Feel free to call him, and see what happens."

"Thank you. I will." Pastor Dave retrieved a piece of paper from under his Bible. "On another note, I hope you don't mind ... I went ahead and compiled a short list of resources I thought might be helpful to you—mainly, support groups. I'm sure your doctor will do the same."

"He already did. He gave me all sorts of information—websites, brochures, phone numbers. He mentioned support groups and also gave me contact information for increasing care as Mom's dementia ... progresses." The lump in her throat returned, and she didn't trust herself to say anything else. How could she tell him she couldn't imagine putting her mom in some special-care home somewhere, regardless of how nice the facility? And even if she could accept the idea her mother might need such a facility at some point, Lilly knew her parents would never be able to afford long-term care.

"All right," the pastor said, handing her his list. "Good. It sounds as if you have plenty of resources to check out, and here are a few you can add. Meanwhile, I'll pray about how and when to try initiating contact with your dad. And, of course, I do want to be able to spend time with your mom whenever I can. I know enough about this disease to realize the importance of maintaining a spiritual life, as much as possible."

When he finished speaking, he got up and walked around his desk to sit down in the chair next to Lilly. Already familiar with the routine, she closed her eyes, bowed her head, and waited.

✵✳✧✧

Rachel was worried. Before Lilly left to return to college the previous day, she had mentioned she'd be back for Thanksgiving, if not before.

Thanksgiving ... already? What am I going to do? How am I going to get to the store and buy everything I need to fix dinner?

Brushing away tears as she sat on the bed in her retro-room, she took in the familiar décor. Seemingly, nearly everything in the room evoked some sort of memory. And strangely enough, each of those memories seemed clearer than the myriad of things Rachel needed to deal with right now. She'd made peace with Lilly's being home so much and hopefully had stopped worrying, feeling more comforted when she was home. If Lilly came a day or so ahead of Thanksgiving, she could help her with the shopping, as well as the cooking.

But who would come to eat with them? Once again taking inventory of the room's many nostalgic items, Rachel remembered large family gatherings for Thanksgiving dinner. "You surely could cook, Mama," she whispered, a smile teasing her lips. "Everyone wanted to come to our house for dinner, just because they knew you were cooking."

She sighed. "I wish I could remember if I ever learned to cook half as well as you. I suppose not, since Pete's always saying something derogatory about my cooking, like the soup isn't warm enough." Tears stung her eyelids, but she ignored them. They came so often these days, fighting her sadness was too much effort. "Sometimes I think the only good thing I ever did was to give birth to my precious Lilly."

That's not all.

The silent voice touched her heart, warming her with promise, knowing immediately who'd spoken to her.

Trembling she whispered, "Father?"

I am here, daughter.

Did she dare ask? Rachel remembered teaching Sunday school once, ages ago, when Lilly was small. What had she done for God lately? She took a deep breath. "What else have I done, Lord? What else have I done to please you?"

If silent words could smile—and evoke a smile from the listener—these words did. *You please me every time you come to spend time with me, to talk with me, to listen to me. You're my child, and you need do nothing else to please me.*

Why did life seem so simple when God spoke to her heart? And why couldn't she hang on to this simplicity throughout the day? God's presence was the only place she would ever find peace. As the days passed, as fear and confusion grew, she desperately needed his peace.

Lilly's heart wrenched with the necessity of the choice. She hated giving up her substitute-teaching job, though she was glad she could retain her part-time writing work, using her laptop wherever she might be. This change also meant giving up the home she had shared with Jacob, the one they had chosen and decorated together ...

But we aren't together anymore. And we never will be again. So I may as well accept reality and get on with my life. Maybe moving back home with Mom and Dad is exactly what I need to do, not only for their sake but also for mine.

She sighed, as she packed up some of her favorite belongings, setting them aside so they wouldn't get mixed up with everything else going into storage. Selling the house would mean splitting the proceeds with Jacob. Yet nothing else made sense, and she imagined Jacob would be happy with the extra money.

That and cutting the last few ties we have to one another. Lilly sighed and grabbed the packing tape to seal up the box. Then she marked it in bold, black letters so there would be no mistake this one would stay with her— wherever she ended up.

Who knows when and where that will be? I suppose everything depends on how things go with my parents.

She opened the bottom drawer of her china cabinet and immediately spotted the large turkey platter she'd purchased for her first *married* Thanksgiving. *We were so happy then. At least, I thought we were. When did that change?*

She shook her head. *No. I'm not going there. These thoughts will accomplish nothing except depress me. And besides, I have work to do if I'm going to take the first steps of moving back to Wildflower.*

The platter called her, and she reached for it. Why not take this with her to her parents' place? After all, Thanksgiving was only a few days away, and she was no doubt going to have to do the majority of the cooking herself. *Might as well incorporate the platter into the event.*

Within the hour, she loaded the car and was ready to go. She sighed at the overwhelming task of going through the rest of her things—many of which were Jacob's and which he would no doubt want—things needing to be done if she were to put the house on the market.

How soon should I list the house? She climbed into the driver's seat and put the key into the ignition. *And who should I list it with? Jacob doesn't even know about any of this yet. If he did, he'd no doubt want to list it with his sister, but I'm not sure I'm comfortable with using her. She and I were friends once. But, as they say, blood is thicker than water.*

She sighed and turned the key. The car immediately purred to life, as another thought popped into her mind. *What if he objects and wants to buy me out so he can move back in?* She shook her head, as if to rid herself of the thought and its accompanying emotions.

Time to go. Though she knew she'd be back—many times—to finish packing and taking care of the numerous details involved in selling a home, leaving, at this moment, seemed as if she were walking away from a huge chunk of her life.

Think Thanksgiving. Focus on getting Mom and Dad through the holiday. Lord knows it's going to take all my time and energy to make that happen. I don't have any time left to dwell on anything else. Mom's Alzheimer's is all I can handle right now.

She sighed and backed out of the driveway. *I'm not even sure I can handle this disease, let alone all the rest. How am I supposed to deal with a mother whose mind is stealing her away bit by bit and a father who's determined to be an invalid, even though the doctor has told him he could most likely regain at least some of his mobility through physical therapy? Mom has waited on him hand and foot since the accident, but she can't continue to dote on him anymore. That leaves me ... and I haven't a clue how I'm going to deal with him on top of everything else.*

Chapter 13

Rachel was determined not to cry, though her emotions were on high alert. Still, she needed to talk to Pete before Lilly arrived, and she knew how much he hated to see her cry.

She sat down on the rocker next to his recliner, where he had plopped down after breakfast and flipped on the TV—his usual morning routine. Pete didn't like to be interrupted during his shows, but this discussion couldn't wait.

"Pete," she said softly. When he didn't respond, she cleared her throat and tried again, this time laying her hand on his arm as she spoke. "Pete, I need to talk with you."

She saw his jaw twitch and knew he'd heard her, though he didn't turn to face her. "About what?" he growled. "I'm watching TV right now. Can't it wait?"

Her initial reaction was to jump up and run to her room in tears. Instead, she forced herself to sit still and take a couple of deep breaths. "Actually," she said, her voice steadier than she had expected, "it can't. Lilly is coming soon, and I want to talk before she gets here."

He punched the mute button on the remote and turned toward her. "About what?"

"About ..." Her coiled nerves threatened to explode and steal even her memories of why she wanted to talk with

Pete. Another deep breath, and she plunged in. "About Lilly. I know she's tried to explain why she's coming home to stay with us, and you know I'm glad she is. But"—she shook her head—"I'm concerned she's giving up her college education, and all because she thinks she needs to be here to help me remember things."

Pete started to speak, and Rachel held up her hand to stop him. "I know. The doctor explained I have Alzheimer's, and I know what that means—at least, most of the time I know. And I know my condition will only get worse." She swallowed the lump in her throat that threatened to unleash a torrent of tears. "For some reason, I can remember Dr. Clark telling me and how I felt when I heard my diagnosis." She shook her head. "But I can't remember much else about that day. I wonder just how much worse I'll be as time goes on."

She brushed away the tears welling in her eyes. "I don't want Lilly to give up her life to take care of me. I truly don't, Pete. Don't we have a choice, some other option?"

At last he spoke. "No, Rachel. We don't have any other options. Lilly's checked into places that take care of people who can't remember things. The cost is ridiculous. We couldn't afford for you to go there, even if we sold this house. And besides, where would I live then? No, we have no choice. Lilly is selling her house and coming back to live with us, to take care of us for as long as we need her."

Rachel tilted her head, confused. "Selling her house? What house? Lilly doesn't have a house. She's still in college."

Pete slammed his hand down on the arm of the chair, and Rachel jumped. "She is *not* still in school, Rachel. She finished college years ago. Don't you remember? We went to her graduation. And then she got married to that no-account Jacob—can't say I'm sorry he's out of the picture now. Don't you at least remember Jacob? The wedding? Any of it?" He leaned toward her. "How about the fact you introduced her to the bum?"

Rachel's heart raced, and her ears began to ring. This was just way too much for her to absorb. Lilly out of college—already? And married? Worse yet, divorced?

Then another thought popped into her mind. She held her breath, afraid to ask but more afraid to hear the answer. "Children?" Her voice was scarcely above a whisper. "Did they have any children? Do we have grandchildren?"

Pete shook his head, his gray eyes telegraphing his sorrow at his previous words. Rachel understood apologizing was hard for Pete—his repentant look was enough. He swallowed before he spoke. One of the few wisps of white hair remaining on his head drooped down onto his forehead. "No grandkids," he said, his voice less gruff. "They were a lot like us—just couldn't seem to have kids."

"But ... we had Lilly."

Pete raised his heavy eyebrows. For a brief moment, Rachel marveled how his eyebrows had more hair than the top of his head. "Not for a long time," he reminded her. "We'd nearly given up when she finally came along. Remember?"

She thought back and realized she did remember, and she was encouraged. "I do," she said. "So why did she and her husband split up? If they'd stayed together and kept trying, like we did, they might have had a child. Then they'd be glad they stayed together."

Pete sighed. "Rachel, Lilly told us their problem wasn't just about not having children, although that was a big issue. Lilly wanted to keep trying, but Jacob didn't. They started fighting and just grew apart." Pete acted frustrated, but Rachel ignored his mood and tried to listen to his words. "Jacob left Lilly and filed for a divorce. Even when Lilly tried to talk to him about getting back together, he wasn't willing. Their divorce is nearly final. They haven't lived together in almost a year, and Lilly has just listed their house with a realtor."

Rachel's heart twisted at the irony—learning her daughter had been married but was getting a divorce. Surely she'd met Jacob several times. According to Pete, she'd even introduced them. Why couldn't she at least remember what he looked like? *So much to take in all at once—not just for me, but for Lilly. What pain she must be in, not being able to have children and then having her husband leave her ... and now this, taking on the care of both her parents. This isn't fair.*

Rachel thought she should say something but couldn't remember what she'd wanted to say. Discouraged and confused, she got up from her chair and headed for the solace of the retro-room. Some time spent there might help put things in perspective.

She'd scarcely touched the guestroom doorknob when she heard the TV come back on. At least for Pete, life had returned to normal.

Rachel couldn't remember exactly how long Lilly had been home ... at least a couple of days. Rachel wondered how Lilly had managed to leave school early and come home several days before Thanksgiving but was glad she did. This meant Rachel wouldn't have to plan and cook the Thanksgiving dinner by herself. For some reason, though she'd done holiday dinners for years without a hitch, the very thought overwhelmed her now.

She glanced at Pete's side of the bed, not surprised he wasn't there. He often got up ahead of her and went to watch TV until she came out and made his breakfast. She should get up and start the coffee before Pete got irritated. He certainly wasn't a patient man—at least not these days.

Rachel lay in bed a few more minutes, listening to the familiar sound of raindrops spattering on the small skylight overhead. More rain. More gray. And there were several months left before she could hope for much of a break.

Why do I know we're in the early stages of another rainy season but not know other things? I can't even remember what other things I don't know! She blinked back tears. *What am I going to do, Lord? How long before I can't remember anything? And then what?* She squeezed her eyes tight. "I keep trying to remember to do the next thing, like Mama taught me," she whispered, "but most of the time, I can't remember what the next thing is."

A lone tear slipped from her eye and trickled down her cheek, landing in her ear. She was about to yield to her feelings and bury her face in the pillow for a good cry when she heard someone in the kitchen. The noise sounded like coffee being made and pots and pans clanking together. Was Lilly up already, making breakfast?

And why wouldn't she be? Rachel checked the illuminated clock on her bed stand. Nearly eight. That was the thing about gray, rainy mornings. Darkness scarcely gave way to light, so judging time was difficult. Thank goodness for illuminated clocks.

She imagined Lilly was used to getting up early for her college classes, so it was only reasonable to think she'd continue her routine since she was home for the Thanksgiving holiday. Rachel smiled, her mind going back to the turkey platter Lilly had given her when she arrived a few days earlier—the only clear memory Rachel had of the day Lilly arrived. *The platter will be perfect for our dinner tomorrow. And Lilly will help in the kitchen, just like she's doing now. She's always been such a help to me, especially cooking meals, and particularly before she left for college. I will be so pleased when she finally graduates. I just hope she decides to move closer to home, so we can spend more time together.*

She got out of bed and slid her feet into her favorite slippers, then reached for her robe at the foot of the bed. The aroma of fresh-brewed coffee called her to the kitchen, drawing her from the darkness that came more often these days—and stayed much longer.

Lilly was restless. She'd made breakfast for her parents and finished cleaning the kitchen. Now she had a little spare time before starting on early preparations for the next day's dinner. Admittedly, since there would be only the three of them, there wasn't much to do at this point. Still, she didn't want to risk leaving anything until the last minute. Sure as she did, her forgetful mother or grouchy father would have some sort of minor meltdown and throw the rest of the day into disarray.

I need to go for a nice long walk. But the raindrops—bordering on sleet and hail—kept her inside. She pictured her treadmill, tucked safely into the corner of her laundry room at home. With the small TV perched on top of the washer, she could exercise while watching a program.

She sighed. *Well, the treadmill isn't going to do me any good there while I'm here.* She decided to go to her room and do some simple calisthenics; on the way, she made a mental note to include the treadmill in her items she needed to bring with her before the home sold, even if she had to make room for it in her parents' garage.

As she made her way down the hall, Mom was heading toward the kitchen. She stopped mid-stride and laid her hand on Lilly's arm.

"Did we already have breakfast?" her mother asked, a frown puckering her forehead. "I don't remember eating, but I'm not hungry."

Lilly smiled. "Yes, Mom, we had breakfast. I'm going to go to my room for a little while now, and then we can make lunch together later. Sound good?"

Mom's frown turned to a smile. "Yes. That sounds very good." Then she continued toward the kitchen.

Lilly watched, pleased her mother smiled so easily. There were times her mother seemed irritated, probably because Mom was frightened she couldn't remember things as she once did.

In the familiarity of her old room, Lilly punched the buttons on her phone until she found some appropriate exercise music. *No more excuses. You have the room to yourself; get to work!*

With a self-directed nod, she began her stretches, transitioning into a mild cardio workout a few minutes later. Though the exercises weren't strenuous, they were enough for her to work up a good sweat. Half an hour later, she no longer felt restless and decided she'd check on her parents.

She wiped the perspiration from her face and went to the TV room, where Dad was sitting in his usual spot. Didn't he ever get sick of sitting in the same chair and watching the same boring programs? *Apparently not.*

"How are you doing, Dad?" she asked, plopping down in the rocker.

Without taking his eyes from the TV, he said, "I could use some more coffee."

Lilly sighed. He'd already had three cups with breakfast, but she supposed another one wouldn't hurt— though she'd have to make a fresh pot. She'd already reached her caffeine limit, but maybe her mom would want another cup too.

She patted Pete's arm. "Coming right up."

As she stepped into the kitchen, Mom sat at the table, her back toward the door, her shoulders hunched as she held her head in her hands. Lilly hurried to her mother's side and knelt down to look up into her face.

"What is it, Mom?" she asked. "Is something wrong? Are you sick?"

Slowly, Mom lifted her head and stared. Seconds passed before her face lit up with recognition. Lilly shivered at the implications.

"Lilly?" Mom asked. "Is that you?"

"Yes, Mom. I'm right here if you need me."

Her mother frowned and tilted her head to one side, the overhead light revealing tears. "How did you get here? Why aren't you in school?"

Lilly had been researching Alzheimer's and knew she needed to keep the answer simple. "Tomorrow's Thanksgiving, remember? I'm here for the holiday weekend."

"Thanksgiving? Oh! I didn't realize ..." She paused for a moment, then said, "I'm so glad you're home. I've missed you."

Lilly gave her mother a hug. "I've missed you too." *And something tells me I'm going to miss you a lot more in the near future, even if I'm right here beside you.* The thought twisted her heart and she nearly lost her composure. For her mother's sake, she needed to stay in control. "The important thing is that I'm here now, and tomorrow we're going to make Thanksgiving dinner together. Won't that be fun?"

Her mother smiled and her eyes brightened as she nodded enthusiastically. "Yes! I can hardly wait." Then she frowned. "But what about the pies? We'll need to make them today so there won't be so much to do tomorrow."

Lilly considered trying to explain she'd picked up a frozen pie at the store and all they had to do was pop it into the oven for an hour, but she thought better of the idea. Once again, she needed to guard against too much information at once. "Sure, Mom. We can make pies this afternoon, after lunch. All right?" Her mother would probably forget this conversation; if not, they'd *make* the frozen pie together.

Her mother's smile returned. "I'm so glad you're home," she said again. "I miss you when you're away at school."

Lilly rose and patted her mom's shoulder. "I'm going to make some more coffee. Dad said he'd like some. How about you?"

Mom's face went blank. "Did I already have some today?"

"A little," Lilly said. "With breakfast. But not so much you can't have another cup now."

"No. Too much coffee gives me heartburn."

"No problem, Mom," Lilly said, mildly surprised her mother remembered about her heartburn. "I'll just make a small pot for Dad."

Before Lilly could get the coffee, she noticed the collection of pill bottles on the table in front of her mother. "What's this?" she asked, picking up a bottle to read the label. She saw the patient's name was Peter Beckwith. Was her mom still doling out her dad's daily pills, even in her condition? Of course she was, and the realization momentarily rocked Lilly.

Before she could voice her concerns, her mother gasped and put her hand over her mouth. "Oh, I forgot about the medicine! I have to fill the daily pill containers for your dad. I think I was just working on that when you came in." The tears returned to her eyes, and she shook her head. "Lilly, I'm so scared. I know I'm supposed to take care of your dad and give him all the right pills at the right time, but"—she sobbed before continuing—"I just can't remember how, even though I think I've been taking care of your father's medicine since the accident." She picked up a bottle in each hand and peered at the labels. "The directions say how often he's supposed to take them, but I can't remember if I already gave them to him or not. And look at this one," she said, shaking one of the bottles. "It's empty. How long ago did we use this one up? I don't even remember how to call the pharmacy to refill them. What if something happens to your dad because I'm not taking care of him the way I should?"

Any tears Mom had been holding back now spilled onto her cheeks, as she once again buried her head in her hands, the way she'd been when Lilly first came into the room.

Why didn't I think of this? Of course Mom can't take care of Dad's medicine anymore. I'll have to handle this. I am so glad I decided to move back in ... for now. She sighed. *This is going to turn into more of a full-time job than I'd realized.*

Chapter 14

Pete was nearly ecstatic. Thanksgiving had arrived, and he could plan on eating an extra special meal, plus he could watch football nearly all day. Could life possibly be any better?

He used the remote to mute the commercial, as he cynically answered his own question. *Yes, life used to be better—a lot better—before the accident. I could come and go as I pleased, work a few more years so I could get a decent retirement ...* He shook his head and sighed. How sad had his life become—he actually got excited about a day with a turkey drumstick and back-to-back football games?

As he took stock of how his life had changed, his joyful mood of a few moments earlier evaporated. Forced to take an early retirement and to settle for partial disability payments, unable to drive or even get around without a walker ... What good was he, anyway?

At least until her mind started going, he'd had Rachel—even if the accident was her fault. He knew she felt guilty and tried to make it up to him by doing everything for him. And why shouldn't she? If she just hadn't insisted on driving that day ...

"Hey, Dad." Lilly interrupted his thoughts as she came in and sat down beside him. "How's the game going?"

Pete looked at his daughter—his only child—and smiled, in spite of himself. She was a beautiful young woman, and talented too. That idiot Jacob didn't deserve her. In fact, Pete realized, if Jacob hadn't skipped out on her, she wouldn't have been able to move back in and help them out. He chuckled. *So the worthless bum did us all a favor. I bet he'd hate to know that.*

Lilly smiled. "What's so funny?"

Pete hadn't realized he laughed out loud. He waved her question away with one hand, as he shook his head. "Nothing," he insisted. "Just ... nothing. And the game's tied up at fourteen. But it's only the third quarter. Anything could happen."

Lilly nodded. "Good. I'm glad you're enjoying your game." She cleared her throat and appeared to be considering something before speaking.

"What?" Pete asked. "Something wrong?"

Lilly raised her eyebrows, but he was certain she was feigning surprise. "Oh, no. Nothing's wrong. Really. I was just ..."

Here it comes. He waited.

She took a deep breath. "This really isn't important and doesn't have to be decided today. But I was just ..."

Get on with it. Spit it out!

"I was talking to the pastor the other day—you know, Pastor Dave, over at Wildflower Community."

Pete nodded impatiently. The commercial was over, and the game was back on.

"Anyway, he might drop by to see Mom one day soon— and you too, of course. Just thought I should let you know before he shows up. So ... he gave me a list of support groups for families of people with Alzheimer's. One of them meets once a week, at a church downtown. Pastor Dave thinks attending might help us adjust to all the changes Mom's going through. After all"—she lowered her voice—"she's going to get much worse, you know."

Oh, really? I hadn't thought of that. I was hoping this was something temporary, like the flu, and she might get over it soon. He didn't want Lilly to hear his sarcastic thoughts so said nothing.

Lilly leaned a bit closer, her eyes searching his. "So, what do you think, Dad?"

"About what?" he barked.

Lilly sighed, and she started to fidget with the fringe on the throw pillow where she sat, though she kept her eyes on him. "About the support group. Do you think we should go?"

He shrugged. "How would I know? But yeah, okay. If you think you should, then go. I'm sure your mom and I can get along by ourselves for an hour or so a week. And sure, if the pastor wants to drop by and see your mother, fine. But tell him not expect to include me in his visits."

Pete tried to ignore the disappointment on his daughter's face, turning instead to the TV and unmuting the sound. "Do whatever you want," he said, effectively ending the conversation.

After a moment, Lilly got up from her chair and left the room.

✶✸✧✧

Somehow the dinner came together without a major hitch. By late afternoon, the three of them were seated around the dining room table, a spot usually reserved for company and special occasions. Rachel decided this qualified for both. Lilly was home from school, visiting for the holiday; and Thanksgiving was certainly a special occasion. So when Rachel noticed her daughter setting the kitchen table, she intervened and suggested they celebrate by sitting in the dining room. "The way we've always done," Rachel said, surprised she could so easily remember this fact, even though she couldn't remember what she'd had for breakfast that day.

Thankfully, Lilly responded enthusiastically. Rachel looked around the table with joy, pleased to see the two people she loved most in the entire world enjoying a delicious meal together.

Rachel picked at her mashed potatoes as she mused over how well the dinner was going. *Lilly really outdid herself. She's actually turned into quite a good cook. How she's managed to do that while she's away at college, I can't imagine. She'll make someone a good wife one day.*

She scolded herself for her sexist thought, then another thought took root. *Grandchildren ... I would love to have grandchildren one of these days. Oh, how I pray Lilly finds a good husband, someone who will love and appreciate her the way she deserves.*

Lilly met Rachel's gaze, and they exchanged smiles. This was turning out to be a lovely day, and Rachel couldn't be happier. *Except, of course, I know Lilly will have to leave on Sunday to go back to school. But only until the Christmas holidays. Then we'll have her for two full weeks.*

Rachel looked at Pete who was bent over his plate, his nearly bald head gleaming in the chandelier's light. He certainly seemed to be enjoying his meal. Rachel almost laughed out loud at the size of the drumstick sitting on his plate. She thought back to previous Thanksgiving dinners they'd shared together. *He'll finish that off in no time. Then he'll have at least one piece of pie, maybe two, before he starts moaning about being so full he can never eat another bite.* This time the chuckle escaped. *But, of course, he'll be back in the kitchen, rummaging through the refrigerator for leftovers, before Lilly and I can finish cleaning up in here.*

Pete raised his head. "What's so funny?"

Rachel shrugged her shoulders. "Oh, I don't know. I was just thinking about all the Thanksgiving dinners we've eaten together over the years—and how you'll be back in the kitchen, looking for leftovers before the day is over."

"Why shouldn't I? That's what Thanksgiving's for, isn't it?"

Wasn't the holiday meant for much more than stuffing oneself? She decided not to say anything. Besides, she'd better get busy eating before her meal got cold.

"The only real difference ..." Pete said, snagging Rachel's attention and leaving his unfinished comment hanging between them.

She raised her head and looked back at him. "What's that, sweetheart?"

"You used to be able to cook the dinner by yourself—and you did a good job too." He shook his head. "But now you can't even boil water without messing it up. I'm glad Lilly's here to keep things going." He glanced at Lilly, who had stopped eating and watched her father, her brown eyes wide.

He turned his attention back to Rachel. "Who knows what would happen if I had to keep counting on you for everything? Things would be a mess for sure." He stuffed a forkful of dressing into his mouth, as if to indicate the end of the discussion.

Tears pricked Rachel's eyes, and this time she knew she couldn't control them. Dropping her fork onto her plate with a clatter, she bolted from her chair and nearly ran down the hallway to her room, tears spilling from her eyes. She overheard Lilly scold her father, but Rachel didn't care. She slammed the bedroom door behind her and threw herself across the bed.

Her daughter had been in twice since Rachel's crying jag erupted, but she ignored Lilly. She wasn't the one who had pierced her mother's heart; Pete did—always Pete. Rachel sighed. How long did she have to put up with such a selfish, ungrateful man? Even the thought she had caused the accident transforming him into the man she scarcely knew didn't help. Of course the accident had been her fault. Did she have to pay every day for the rest of her life?

Besides, haven't I done everything humanly possible to atone for the accident?

The answer came unexpectedly, sending a chill down her spine, then immediately covering her in warmth. *That's the problem. You've done everything humanly possible, and nothing has been enough. Nothing you do will ever be enough. You can't change or fix this, daughter... but I can.*

Rachel's tears slowed to a trickle, as she fought the inclination to ignore what she'd heard, to write the thought off as her wild imagination and unstable brain going off on another tangent. She knew better. She'd heard the voice before, and he'd never lied to her.

"I know you're right, Lord," she whispered. "And I'm sorry." She swallowed and brushed at the remaining tears on her face, then sat up on the bed. "Why do I keep trying to fix the unfixable?"

I didn't say your situation is unfixable. I said you can't change what has already happened.

"Then what ...?"

What else did I say?

She paused, squinting her eyes as if to better concentrate, to pull up the words he'd spoken.

"You said,"—she took a deep breath—"you said I couldn't fix the situation with Pete, but—but you can."

Exactly. So when are you going to give your situation to me so I can help?

"I'm not sure I know how to give this to you," she admitted, as much to herself as to God.

I can take care of your uncertainty too. All I need from you is a willing heart.

For several moments, Rachel sat on the edge of the bed, listening to her own breaths as they became more relaxed and even. She knew he was waiting.

She hung her head. "I am willing," she whispered. "Help me, Father."

Peace flooded her heart then, and though her mind still argued with her about the decision she'd made, she sensed her heart would win out.

She stood to her feet. "Today is Thanksgiving," she told herself. "Go out there so you can spend what's left of the holiday with your family. After all, isn't this what Mama would say—'do the next thing?'" She took a deep breath and walked into the bathroom to wash her face.

Chapter 15

"I know you're right, Dad. We all know you're right. If Mom hadn't insisted on driving the day of the accident, you wouldn't be on a walker today. But she did, and you are, and at some point, you need to accept your life and stop blaming her. Besides, I'm not convinced you need to use a walker, even now."

Rachel stopped in the hallway, listening to the conversation between her daughter and her husband, not feeling in the least guilty about eavesdropping. Lilly's words seemed to confirm what Rachel had heard from the Lord just minutes earlier. *What happened … happened. Now leave things there and move on, allowing God to bring the healing with time.*

"That's easy for you to say," Pete groused. "You're not the one who wakes up with pain in your legs, then spends the day in pain until nighttime—counting on pills to help you sleep. Do you really think I like being dependent on pain pills and pushing this walker around everywhere I go?"

Lilly paused before answering. "Actually, Dad, sometimes I do. I mean, the doctor told you after the accident you could probably regain at least some of your leg strength—and ease the pain in the process—if you'd just go to therapy. So why don't you? I'm here now, and I can take you."

Rachel imagined Pete shaking his head. "No. I am not going to let my daughter drive me around like I'm some sort of invalid. Even if I was willing to go to therapy—and I'm not saying I am—I'm not going to have you take me there. You're here to help your mother, not me. So how would I even get there? We sure don't have any extra money for me to call a cab or Uber several times a week."

The irony of Pete's words wasn't lost on Rachel. *Like he's some sort of invalid? That's exactly what he is, and yet he seems to want to be. He's not going to let Lilly help him get better any more than he's let me these last few years. He'd rather sit in his chair and waste his life watching TV and demanding someone bring him whatever he wants or needs.* Rachel sighed. Their situation had never been clearer than at this moment. God's words echoed in her heart. *I'm the only one who can remedy your situation.*

The question in Rachel's mind now was how Lilly would respond to her father's stubborn refusal to accept the obvious. She didn't have long to wait to find out.

"Fine," Lilly said. "So you won't let me take you to therapy, and you say you and Mom don't have any extra money for cabs or anything else. I know this part's true, Dad. Neither you nor Mom had good pension plans, so you have to live mostly on Social Security and your small amount of disability. But maybe there are other options."

"For instance?"

"Well ... how about a reverse mortgage? That would free up some money for all sorts of things, including any extra care Mom might need as her disease worsens."

"I thought you were going to stay here and take care of her."

"I am. But, Dad, we don't know how bad things will get or what else she may need in the future. Alzheimer's care can be really expensive."

Rachel held her breath as she waited to hear Pete's answer. "Well, we're not going to pay for her needs with our house. We bought this place just a few years after we married, and it's paid for. I'm not about to borrow against it now."

"That's not what I'm saying," Lilly argued, and Rachel could tell her daughter was struggling to control her frustration. "A reverse mortgage isn't a typical loan, Dad. It's—"

"I don't care what a reverse mortgage is," Pete said, interrupting Lilly before she could say another word. "We're not doing anything with this house, period. Do you understand?"

When neither spoke again, the conversation seemed to have come to an abrupt halt. Rachel pressed herself against the wall, as she saw Lilly storm out of the TV room, on her way to the kitchen. Pete, on the other hand, must have punched the remote, because the sounds of a football game quickly filled the painful silence.

The day after Thanksgiving, Lilly once again found herself sitting across the desk from Pastor Dave. She was beginning to feel like she was spending more time in church these last few weeks than she had in years. But she really didn't know where else to turn, obviously needing outside support if she were to get through all this.

Whatever this might be. And I know it's a lot more than Mom having Alzheimer's.

She twisted the strap on her purse as she waited for the pastor to bring her a cup of coffee. She really didn't need any, but discussing her family's circumstances was easier when she had something to keep her hands busy. She released her grip on her purse strap just as Pastor Dave held out a cup of steaming, hot liquid, which she gratefully accepted.

"So catch me up on what's going on," Pastor Dave said as he sat back down across from her, his own cup in hand. "Anything new? How was Thanksgiving?"

Lilly sighed. "Thanksgiving was all right, I guess." She stopped and shook her head. "No, not really. Some of the day was, but some was awful." She paused and tried to bring her unruly thoughts into order. "Everything started out okay, I suppose. In fact, the meal came together surprisingly well. Mom helped me in the kitchen, Dad watched football on TV, and the meal was fine. But then ..."

Pastor Dave set his cup down and leaned forward, his elbows resting on the desk. Lilly sensed he was giving her his full attention, which she appreciated.

As she explained her father's insensitivity at the dinner table and her mother's subsequent meltdown, she saw the growing compassion in Pastor Dave's eyes. She suddenly felt free to show her feelings, and tears quickly followed.

Pastor Dave passed her an open box of tissues. She dabbed at her eyes and reminded herself not to wear mascara the next time she came to see this kind man. By the time she'd finished detailing the day, she was exhausted.

The pastor seemed to understand. "Must have been incredibly difficult," he said. "I know you love both your parents, and you're caught in the middle of their conflict." He sighed. "I wish I could encourage you by saying things will get better, but I think we both know your mother's situation will only worsen. How quickly, we don't know; but we need to prepare for the worst. And since your father doesn't seem able—or willing—to try to understand and help with your mom's increased care needs, we'll have to plan as if you'll be carrying the full load."

Lilly's sigh was almost a sob. "I'm afraid you're right. I'm an only child, my husband is long gone, and I have no children of my own. Though, if I did, children could complicate the matter even more. I certainly couldn't devote nearly all my time to Mom if I had little ones to care for. I've already quit my substitute teaching job and just work on some freelance writing assignments when I can." Tears bit her eyes again. "I guess that's the main reason I'm here. I don't know if I can do this alone."

Pastor Dave got up, then came around the desk to sit beside her. "Nor should you have to," he said, his voice soothing. "I will certainly continue to pray for all of you and to be here if you need someone to talk to. But you need more than I can give you, Lilly. You need God, and you need others—others who can share your painful journey because they too are on similar paths."

He handed her another tissue. "I've been considering the various support groups on the list I gave you, and I think the one best suited for you is the Thursday evening group at Spirit of Joy Church downtown. Many of those who attend are Christians, so you'd have an added connection—assuming you still believe and have a relationship with Christ."

Lilly felt the heat crawl up her neck into her cheeks. In spite of the fact she too had singled out that particular support group as her primary choice, she hadn't expected these questions from the pastor. Did she still believe in all she'd been taught as a child? Did she still have a relationship with God? If not, did she even want one? "I'm not sure what I believe right now," she ventured. "Will I still be able to attend this group?"

Pastor Dave shook his head. "Yes, of course. I said many in the group are believers but certainly not all. However, all are caregivers for someone with Alzheimer's and/or dementia. In fact, I imagine you'll find several who are about the same age as you, since adult children often inherit the primary care for a parent with this condition." He paused. "Would you like the contact information for the group? I think their number was on the list I gave you before, but I can give it to you again now."

Lilly hesitated, then nodded. "Yes, please. I feel like I'm drowning, trying to do this by myself."

Pastor Dave smiled. "Then I definitely think this group is exactly what you need. Not only will they be a great support to you emotionally and spiritually, but they'll also have other resource information for you, which is always helpful."

Lilly nodded again, the lump in her throat preventing her from speaking.

"All right," Pastor Dave said, taking her hands. "Let's pray, and then I'll get the information for you from Kelly. Please keep in mind the greatest support and resource—for this or any other difficult situation—is God. He cares for your mother even more than you or I, and he cares for you too. More than you can ever imagine."

He prayed as tears trickled down Lilly's face.

Rachel sang while in the shower, "I'll fly away, oh glory …" The tune had run through her mind since she first awoke. *Probably because today is Sunday. But also because Lilly is coming with me to church. I remember how much she loved going to church when she was little. Oh, Lord, please draw her back to you! I know she drifted away when she was in her teens, and now she's in college … No. That's not right.* Rachel tried to understand what wasn't right but couldn't. Ah well, she'd figure out what was wrong later. For now she simply needed to *do the next thing*, which today was to finish getting ready for church.

By the time she finished dressing and opened the bedroom door to step out into the hallway, the heady aroma of freshly made coffee and fried bacon greeted her. *Lilly is spoiling you.* Rachel smiled as she headed toward the kitchen *Lilly will no doubt have to leave to get back to school today, so we may as well enjoy the last breakfast she'll make for us until she comes home at Christmas.*

As Rachel passed the TV room, Pete was already ensconced in his usual spot. She frowned. Couldn't he at least join them in the kitchen for breakfast?

She was about to confront him on the subject when Lilly called out, "Breakfast is ready. Come and eat."

An irritated look settled on Pete's face as he hoisted himself from the chair and grabbed his walker, and ambled toward the kitchen. When he saw Rachel, he grunted a one-syllable greeting and pushed past her. With a sigh, Rachel followed.

"Good morning!" Lilly was already dressed for church, wearing one of Rachel's old aprons, as she poured orange juice and coffee for the three of them. "Bacon and eggs are coming," she announced, as Pete and Rachel took seats around the table.

"It smells wonderful," Rachel said, smiling appreciatively at her daughter. "You've turned into quite a cook while you've been away." She frowned. "I truly can't imagine how you found time to cook while going to school, though. Still, those skills will serve you well once you've graduated."

Pete shook his head as Lilly scooped scrambled eggs onto their plates.

"Thank you, Mom. I enjoy cooking, especially for you and Dad." She chuckled. "You probably thought I'd never learn my way around the kitchen. I sure wasn't any good at cooking while I was growing up."

Rachel thought otherwise but kept quiet. Pete snagged several pieces of crisp bacon from the platter in the middle of the table. She thought she should caution him to watch his cholesterol but decided against saying anything. She didn't want to make Lilly feel bad.

"So, Dad," Lilly said, stirring creamer into her coffee, "why don't you come to church with me and Mom this morning? You haven't been in ages."

Pete looked up from his plate, a dark scowl on his face. "No, I haven't," he growled, "and since when is my church attendance any business of yours? It's not like you go regularly either."

Lilly's cheeks flushed, and her smile faded. "You're right, Dad. Sorry. I just thought I'd ask."

"You asked," he grunted, "and I answered. So let's eat."

Rachel ached for her daughter. The girl's generous heart was so easily wounded, and she hadn't meant to irritate Pete. Should she say something to ease the situation? Instead, she reached under the table to pat Lilly's leg. Her smile assured Rachel she'd made the right decision.

The food was delicious, and Rachel was full before she could finish half of the eggs her daughter had heaped on her plate. She tried to eat a bit more, then had to confess she couldn't eat another bite. Lilly was gracious and began to clear the table.

"We'll leave in about fifteen minutes," Lilly said, as she carried dishes to the sink. "You might want to bring a jacket, Mom. It's cool out there, and it looks like rain."

"This is the Pacific Northwest," Pete said, pushing himself up from the table. "It always looks like rain. And you take a jacket wherever you go."

With that, he exited the room, while Rachel stood up to see if she could help her daughter clean the kitchen before they left.

Chapter 16

Rachel excused herself to take a nap, her thoughts in a whirl as she lay on her bed. *How strange. I can't remember what I just had for lunch, but I can remember nearly every detail of Pastor Dave's sermon, especially the Scripture references. I don't understand, Lord; but I do so appreciate your help. If I forget everything else but remember you, that's really all that matters, isn't it?*

She sensed God's smile, even as she heard him whisper to her heart. *Exactly. And don't worry, daughter. I will seal to your memory the important things. If you forget the rest, it's all right. I will carry you in the palm of my hand.*

More and more lately, even as she fought the overwhelming panic, she sensed God's presence in a deeper and more powerful way than ever before. *I truly feel you have me in the palm of Your hand, Father. When I concentrate on this truth, the fear goes away.* She smiled. *And then I hear "I'll Fly Away" in my mind, and I can hardly wait until you carry me home.*

She listened expectantly for his response, and she wasn't disappointed. *Trust me to do exactly what is needed at just the right time. Until then, you can be sure I have a purpose for you, plans to bless you and those around you. Can you hang on to this promise?*

Rachel sighed. *I will try, Lord. But please help me when I fail ... which seems so often these days.* Tears pricked her eyes, as she sensed his nearness.

All else may fail, but my word will never fail, and my love will never abandon you.

As his words washed over her, flooding her heart with peace, she closed her eyes and drifted off to sleep.

Lilly's heartbeats hammered in her ears. One week since Thanksgiving, and what was she doing? How could this possibly help her care for her mother? She'd argued with herself all day, hoping to find a legitimate excuse to change her plans.

I guess I didn't succeed because here I am. She pulled into the church parking lot, surprised she had no problem finding a parking space, though she chastised herself. *I thought there'd be lots of people here by now. Since there are only two other cars besides mine, that's obviously not the case.*

Once she'd turned off the engine, she sat quietly for several minutes. Two more cars arrived during that time, but only one person got out of each. She glanced at the luminescent face on her watch. *Five to seven. If I'm going to do this, I guess I'd better get moving.* She took a deep breath and opened the car door.

The church was an older building, located in the downtown area, where the community of Wildflower first began. Pastor Dave had told her there had been at least two other congregations in the church before a non-denominational group moved in and named the fellowship Spirit of Joy.

The church's history is interesting, but I'm here to learn as much as I can about caring for someone with Alzheimer's. I don't plan on becoming best friends with any of these people.

The front door was open, so she stepped inside the foyer, which she could see led to the sanctuary. A sign greeted her, showing the name of the support group and meeting room. An arrow helped point the way.

Lilly walked down the hall, reassured she was heading in the right direction, as the sound of people talking and laughing drew her on. Another sign outside an open classroom door welcomed her and once again announced the name of the group meeting there tonight.

This is the room. Pasting a stiff smile on her face, she stepped inside. Half a dozen people—four women and two men—stood in a circle in front of a long table, where coffee and donuts awaited. Not interested in anything to eat or drink, Lilly took a seat at the end of the sixth row. *This way I can maintain at least a modicum of anonymity.*

She placed her keys inside her purse, then looked up to find an attractive, gray-haired woman smiling down at her.

"Welcome," the woman said, extending her hand. "I'm Lena."

Wishing there were a gracious way to ignore her but knowing there wasn't, Lilly took the woman's hand. "I'm Lilly," she said, forcing a half-smile.

"Can I offer you a cup of coffee and a donut?" Lena asked.

Lilly shook her head. "Oh, no, thank you. I just ate."

Lena nodded. "Okay. Then why don't you come up front and join us?" She glanced at her watch, then back at Lilly. "We're just about ready to start."

Reluctantly, Lilly followed the woman, who looked to be about her mother's age, to the front of the room.

Lena indicated a circle of chairs in the front left corner of the room. "Sit anywhere you'd like," she said.

Lilly wondered why she hadn't noticed them before. She thought she had been sitting where she liked when she was six rows back, but apparently this wasn't how things were done here. She took a seat in the circle, then looked up to find three more people had drifted in, talking and laughing like old friends. They made their way to the coffee and donuts table, then joined her in the circle of chairs while Lilly did her best to look preoccupied with finding something in her purse.

"Welcome, everyone," Lena called out, gesturing for the last of the stragglers to join them. "We're so glad you've come."

Lilly looked up, and her eyes locked with Lena's. The woman's smile was contagious, and Lilly felt herself returning the gesture, despite the fact she was still convinced she'd made a mistake coming to the meeting. What could these people possibly know about caring for those with Alzheimer's or dementia she hadn't already learned from her extensive online research?

"We have a new face with us tonight," Lena announced. "Please, everyone, greet Lilly and make her feel welcome."

Lilly felt her cheeks flame at the unwanted attention, yet she couldn't deny the group's warmth and friendliness, as they all made a point to say hello and to welcome her into their midst.

At last the attention turned from Lilly to Lena, as the older woman asked those who felt comfortable doing so to stand and join hands for an opening prayer. Lilly hesitated, not comfortable at all. Since everyone else had formed a circle, she decided she would rather join them than show what an outsider she truly believed herself to be.

The prayer was short but heartfelt, not nearly as painful as Lilly had feared. Lena opened the prayer, but then allowed others to join in as they wished. Three others did so, all of them thanking God for his love and for the group and then they all returned to their seats.

Now what? Is this like some AA meeting, where we have to stand up and say how long it's been since we felt frustrated and on the verge of tears, trying to care for a loved one who grows more and more distant with each passing day? If that were the case, then she'd gone as far as she was going to with this group. She'd listen to their stories, but she wasn't ready to share hers.

Thankfully, no one called on her to speak, though she recognized she was free to do so. Instead, she listened to several of the others, who shared their experiences over the past week. Lilly had to admit she was surprised at how similar many of those experiences were to her own. The one thing that stood out the most to her, something she filed away in her memory and then considered as she drove home later that evening, was how the group members referred to themselves as "care-partners" rather than "caregivers."

Lena had even taken the time to explain why. "Calling ourselves care-partners helps keep our loved ones on an equal plane with us. We are partners together in this difficult journey, and we need to allow our loved ones to maintain as much dignity and respect as possible. Calling ourselves caregivers, though perhaps an appropriate term, puts our loved ones in the position of being receivers—or takers—only. We believe treating them as partners helps us all relate to one another more respectfully."

The explanation made a lot of sense. Lilly decided, as her mother's situation progressed, she would do her best to help Mom think of herself as a partner and not just a taker. The thought made losing her mother to such an awful disease only slightly less difficult.

✦✳✧❖

His own snoring woke him. Pete sat up, blinked, and shook his head to regain his bearings. Then he reprimanded himself for not knowing exactly where he'd be at any given time: if not in bed, then in front of the TV. How had he allowed his life to be reduced to such a small and meaningless schedule?

This isn't my fault. If Rachel hadn't insisted on driving that day, none of this would have happened. I would still have the pleasant, normal life I had up until then. No. This life I have now is definitely not my fault.

A commercial ended, and the sounds of a game filled the air. *Of course. Monday night football. Well, at least this is one of the better segments of my otherwise empty life. Of course, the season will be over in a few weeks, and then what? Back to game shows or reality programs?*

He heard voices, separate from the announcers on TV. *Rachel and Lilly, in the kitchen, cleaning up after dinner.* He sighed. If he was honest with himself, he'd have to admit, even before the accident, he often felt like odd-man-out in their family trio. *I guess this is normal, though. How does a guy compete with two women who have such different interests than his? Still, my life has gotten worse since the accident.*

He heaved a sigh. *There I go again. Dividing everything in my life between the before and after of the accident, as if my life ended when we were broadsided. Now I'm just marking time until I check out permanently.*

And then what? The question he'd asked himself a lot lately. Since he didn't much like the answer he came up with, he ignored them. And tonight was no exception. He wasn't about to send his thoughts into a deep, seemingly never-ending spiral.

The announcer caught his attention when he said something about one of the players having been injured a few weeks earlier. Apparently, he was having some memory issues, although the doctors assured him the memory loss was temporary.

Wish I could say this was true for Rachel. He sighed so deeply he shuddered. Was God punishing her for being so stubborn and causing her husband to incur such a debilitating injury? No. He might not know God well … if at all … but Pete was certain a deity did not behave in such a way.

More than I can say for myself. I know I need to forgive Rachel, but I just can't seem to let go of my anger. I know she feels hurt when I blame her, and my attitude sure doesn't help. But how do I get past my annoyance when I have to push myself around on a walker every time I need to get up for any reason? He shook his head again. *Maybe that's why I spend so much time in this blasted chair, watching whatever I can find on TV. At least if I'm sitting down, I don't focus quite as much on being crippled—well, almost crippled.*

He interrupted his own thoughts to watch the opposing team's quarterback heave a last-minute Hail-Mary in hopes of scoring before halftime. The effort failed, and Pete was relieved. He was counting on his team winning, which would nearly ensure them a berth in the upcoming playoffs.

For the most part, he ignored the halftime show until the station showed an interview with one of the injured players who talked about how hard he was working at physical therapy so he could return to the game. A hot slice of guilt pierced Pete's heart. *Why do I feel like he's talking to me, like I'm not willing to do the hard work I need to so I can get back in the game of life?*

Irritated, he muted the sound for the remainder of the interview.

Chapter 17

Lilly was making coffee Tuesday morning when her phone rang. She didn't recognize the number on caller I.D., but the area code indicated the call was local. "Hello?"

"Lilly? This is Pastor Dave. How are you?"

She frowned. Had she forgotten an appointment? She didn't think so. "I'm fine, thanks. What can I do for you, Pastor?"

"I hope I'm not calling at an inconvenient time. I wanted to run something by you before I follow through. I'm thinking of coming to visit your dad. I know we talked about me coming to visit your mom and maybe including your dad too, but I don't think we came to any clear decision. I've given the idea a lot of prayer lately, and I'd like to try to visit with your dad without you or your mom there—if you think it's all right, of course. What do you think? Would he be open to a chat?"

Lilly lowered her voice. "I'm not sure. I hope so, but you never know with Dad." She paused. "So you don't want to see Mom?"

"Oh, of course. And I will. Right now, I sense the need to make meeting with your dad a priority." He hesitated with an audible, deep breath. "I also wondered if you would take your mom somewhere before I come over. I think your dad might be more receptive if he isn't trying to save face in front of you or your mom."

"You could be right. I often wonder how much of Dad's bravado is just part of his façade. Even his grumpiness might ease if Mom and I aren't here. So yes ... sure, I'd be glad to take Mom somewhere. Out to lunch, maybe."

She could almost see Pastor Dave smile. "Perfect. How about tomorrow? And do you think I should call ahead or just show up?"

Lilly thought for a moment. "Again, I'm not sure, although stopping by might be best. That way he won't have a chance to tell you not to come, which I imagine he would if you call and ask him. Of course, there's no guarantee he'll even answer the door ... or if he does, he'll invite you in. But I'd say your chances are better if you don't call first."

"I was leaning in that direction myself. So what's a good time?"

"I'll tell Dad I'm taking Mom out to lunch. He won't mind a bit so long as we leave him something to eat while we're gone. Mom and I will leave a little before noon and be gone for a couple hours. Does that work for you?"

"Perfect. Thanks, Lilly. And please, pray your dad will be open to talking with me, will you?"

Maybe she should remind Pastor Dave she wasn't in the habit of praying. Then again, she might be praying about the pastor's visit after all. She really hoped Dad would be open to talking about his wife's condition. Who knew? God just might be listening.

✹ ❋ ✪ ✧

Rachel's fingers shook slightly as she buttoned her favorite blue blouse. Lilly had asked to go out to lunch, promising to fix Pete's lunch for him before they left. "Mom, you can even choose the restaurant," Lilly had said.

Rachel smiled. No problem. She'd just the other day been thinking about the fish place downtown. She hadn't been there in ages, and eating there with Lilly would be so nice.

Finished with the buttons, Rachel stood in front of the mirror hanging on the back of her bedroom door. She scarcely recognized herself anymore. How had she aged so quickly? Her short hair still maintained its reddish-brown hues, but patches and streaks of gray seemed to be taking over. And those bags under her eyes! When had they snuck in?

The same time your chin started to sag. She nearly laughed at the irony. Whether or not she remembered when those first signs of old age had shown up didn't matter. They were there, and they weren't going away any time soon. "Not in this life, anyway," she whispered.

True, came the reply within her heart. *But when you come home to be with me, all your wrinkles will disappear. Illness and old age will no longer have a claim on you.*

She imagined her heavenly Father standing beside her, speaking to her with such words of love. How could she be afraid of what tomorrow would bring, when she knew her eternal destiny was set in stone? *In the Cornerstone, to be exact.*

Grabbing her purse, she opened the door and made her way down the hallway toward the front door and grabbed her coat and scarf from the closet. "I'm ready," she called out, then waited.

In a matter of seconds, Lilly came up beside her, carrying a plate with a sandwich and chips. "I just need to take this to Dad," she said, "and then we can go."

Rachel smiled. Lilly was always so thoughtful. "I'm going to miss you when you go back to school."

For a moment, Lilly seemed at a loss for words. "I'll be right back," she finally said, then turned and went to the TV room, where the noise of a game show assured Rachel her husband was in his usual spot. She hoped he'd be happy with his lunch and not resent them for going out without him.

Though, he wouldn't go even if we invited him. She shook her head. *I can't remember the last time he wanted to go out and eat—or anywhere else, for that matter. Before the accident, I suppose.*

She sighed. There was nothing she could do about the situation now, so she might as well push the thought from her mind and concentrate on having a wonderful outing with her daughter.

Despite the gray overcast and drippy weather, Rachel was grateful to be sitting across from her daughter at a lovely little restaurant on the coast. The drive over had been pleasant and uneventful, except for the mix-up about the restaurant.

Rachel shook her head, as she stared out the window at the frothy waves, swirling and crashing less than two hundred yards away. "I just don't understand," she said, without turning her head to look at Lilly. She was still confused about what had happened to the fish place, her favorite for years. "I'm sure Pete and I had dinner there just the other day. It's always been our favorite spot. The fish and chips are the best anywhere."

Lilly smiled as she turned toward Rachel, lightly squeezing her hand. "I know, Mom. I've forgotten similar things too. Change comes quickly sometimes. No telling when the place closed its doors." Lilly's smile widened. "But look around, Mom. Everything turned out for the best, right? We're going to get our fish and chips here, and I'm sure our lunch will be delicious. And we certainly have a beautiful view, don't we?"

Rachel smiled and looked back out the window. "That's true, sweetheart. I can only imagine how nice the view would be when the sun's out—better yet, watching the sunset at the end of a clear day."

Lilly patted Rachel's hand. "Then let's make a date to come here for dinner on the first sunny day we have. Even if we have to wait until next summer."

Rachel smiled. "You could be right. Maybe your dad will even come with us."

Their meals arrived then, and they turned their attention to some excellent fish and chips, speaking only occasionally as they ate. Halfway through her meal, Rachel laid her fork down and smiled. "The meal was wonderful," she said, "but I'm stuffed. I can't eat another bite."

"I'm almost there myself," Lilly said. "Next time our waitress passes by, I'll ask her for some takeout boxes."

Rachel glanced out the window again, pleased the rain seemed to have stopped. Off to the left, a light shone through a break in the clouds. "I truly would like to bring your father here," she said, still staring out the window. "I know he'd like the view, and he adores fish and chips." She turned to Lilly. "Next time we'll bring him along."

Lilly nodded. "Sounds like a great idea."

Rachel's heart fell then, as she realized her daughter needed to get back to school soon. "When do you leave?"

Lilly frowned. "Leave for where, Mom?"

"For school, of course. You've been home a lot lately, and you can't keep missing so much school. So when do you go back?"

Lilly appeared uncomfortable, as she hesitated before answering. "I'm not sure, Mom. But I'll let you know soon, all right? In the meantime, let's enjoy our time together, shall we?"

Rachel sighed. "Of course, sweetheart. I just wish your dad would join us now and then. He spends entirely too much time in front of the TV. That can't be good for him."

"You're right. Let's see if we can convince him to get out with us soon, even for a short ride. What do you think?"

"I think that's a wonderful idea. I worry about him, not having any interests or friends or ..." Her voice drifted off. "He's probably sitting in front of the TV right now, eating his lunch." She frowned. "We did leave him something to eat, didn't we?"

Lilly patted her mother's hand again. "Yes, Mom, we did. Don't worry. He's fine."

Rachel wanted to believe this was true, but she couldn't. In fact, she didn't believe Pete had been fine since before the accident. "Do you think we should get back and check on him soon? We've been gone quite a while ... haven't we?"

"Not too long," Lilly assured her. "And we'll leave as soon as we pay the bill and get those takeout boxes."

Rachel nodded absently, her mind still on her husband, sitting all alone in front of the TV.

Chapter 18

Pete tried to ignore the doorbell, but whoever stood at the front door was persistent. He sighed and pushed himself out of his seat and onto his walker. *Probably some salesman. Well, I'll give him a piece of my mind and send him packing.*

The bell sounded again as Pete stopped in front of the door. Shaking his head and prepared to fire a round at whoever was there, Pete pulled the door open, stopping when his walker got in the way.

A somewhat tall middle-aged man with dark hair and eyes peered at him through the screen door. "Mr. Beckwith?"

"Who wants to know?" Pete growled. "If you're selling something, you might as well turn around right now and walk away, because I'm not buying."

The man smiled. "I'm not selling anything, I assure you. I'm Pastor Dave Barnett from Wildflower Community. I know you haven't seen me in a while, but I haven't changed that much, have I?"

Pete's irritation at what he considered a sideswipe by the pastor, intimating Pete hadn't darkened the doors of their church in years, was overshadowed only by his surprise at seeing the man standing on their front porch.

"If you're looking for Rachel, she's out having lunch somewhere with our daughter." He gripped the doorknob, ready to close it and return to his TV program. "I'll let them know you were looking for them."

"Actually, I wasn't looking for them at all. I came by, hoping to get a chance to visit with you for a few minutes."

The pastor stood his ground, smiling hopefully. Pete's hand remained on the door. He itched to close it, and then he'd walk away.

Dave Barnett took one step closer to the screen. "May I come in, Pete? Just for a few minutes."

Pete hesitated, then sighed. "Fine." He took his hand from the doorknob, opened the screen, pulled the walker close, and stepped back to let the pastor into the entryway. "But not for long. I'm busy right now."

Pete was about to direct the pastor to the TV room, but since he'd just opened his big mouth and said he was busy, he didn't want his guest to realize he hadn't been busy at all. Grateful he'd muted the TV before answering the front door, he led Pastor Dave into the kitchen and offered him a seat at the table.

"I was just about to make some coffee," he said, hoping he could find both the coffee and filters if the pastor took him up on his offer. "Would you like some?"

Dave smiled. "That would be nice. But you said you were busy. I don't want to take up too much of your time."

Pete waved him off. "Don't worry," he said, opening two cupboards before locating the items he needed to get the brew going. "It doesn't take long to drink a cup of coffee." *What was I thinking, letting him inside? I'll probably never get rid of him.*

Pete took his coffee black and couldn't see any point in drinking it any other way, so he didn't offer the pastor any cream or sugar. As the coffee dripped slowly—more slowly than he'd ever realized—into the pot, Pete took a seat at the table, directly across from Pastor Dave.

"So, what have you been working on?" the pastor asked.

Pete lifted his eyebrows, confused. "What do you mean?"

"You said you were busy when I arrived."

"Ah." Pete cleared his throat. "Yeah, I ..." He thought of the jigsaw puzzle in the corner of the TV room, something Lilly had thought might entertain him and give him an alternative to TV. He hadn't even opened the box yet. Besides, putting together a puzzle didn't exactly count as being *busy*. He was going to have to do better than a puzzle.

"Actually, I ..." A picture of himself the one time he'd agreed to try physical therapy popped into his mind, and gave him an idea. "I was doing some physical therapy, a routine they gave me to do at home."

Pastor Dave smiled. "That's great! I'm glad to hear you're exercising. You must be doing better then."

Better than what? Pete swallowed the retort. "I guess so."

The beep told Pete the coffee was finally ready, so he quickly excused himself to pour a couple of cups. Then he realized he was going to have to carry the coffee, one cup at a time, in one hand and scoot the walker back to the table with the other. He cursed silently and tried to figure out an easier way to get the two cups of coffee to the table.

Before he could come up with anything, Pastor Dave stood at his elbow, reaching for the cups. "Here, let me get those," he said.

Pete wanted to turn him down and tell him he didn't need any help, but thanks to his wife's insistence she drive, he was now on a walker and actually did need the help. Wordlessly, he followed the pastor back to the table.

"Just the way I like my coffee," the pastor said, as he took a sip after sitting down. "Hot and strong. None of that sugary, creamy stuff to kill the taste."

Pete's eyebrows went up again. So at least the man knew a good cup of coffee when he drank one. "Yeah, that's the way I like it too, and so does Lilly—most of the time. But she's as bad as her mother when they go to one of those fancy, schmancy coffee shops they have on every corner now. They order some sweet, sugary thing that costs almost as much as I used to make in an hour when I was still working."

Pastor Dave grinned. "I know what you mean. My wife's the same way. And don't even get me started on my two teenaged daughters. They wouldn't dream of drinking coffee not made by a barista." He rolled his eyes and laughed.

Pete chuckled too, surprising himself. But he understood. Lilly was no longer a teenager, but he still remembered how finicky she'd been about certain things.

"So, Pete"—Pastor Dave took another swig of coffee—"what are you doing this Saturday?"

Pete frowned. "Saturday? I don't know. Pretty much the same thing I always do. Why?"

Dave shrugged. "Oh, I don't know. Just a thought. Every other Saturday, some of the men from church get together and have an early breakfast and then go out into the community to help some of our neighbors with things, like leaky faucets, overgrown yards—stuff like that."

"I don't get it. You mean they just go out and knock on doors and ask if people need something done?"

"Not exactly," Pastor Dave said. "Actually, we arrange the visits before Saturday. People at the church know we do this, and they can sign up if they need help. We get a lot of single moms and elderly people—especially widows— who can't quite get everything done themselves. If we hear of people in the community who don't attend our church but who might need similar assistance, we check ahead. If they're interested, we add them to the list."

Pete grunted. He supposed what the pastor said made sense—for church guys, anyway. But he hadn't been a church guy in a very long time ... if ever ... and he wasn't interested in being one now. "No, thanks," he said. "I don't think I can make your breakfast. Besides, how much help could I be on a walker?"

Pastor Dave smiled. "You could come for breakfast, I think you might be surprised at how much help you could be to someone in real need."

Yeah? Well, what about me? Don't I look like someone in need? He shook his head, dismissing the words. "Nah," he said. "I really don't think so. Besides, I don't even drive anymore, and Lilly and I just convinced Rachel not to drive anymore either. In fact, we had to take her keys away. She was getting lost, forgetting where she was going. You know what I mean. So, I just don't see how I could come."

"I could pick you up. It's not out of my way at all."

Pete clenched his jaw. Now what? He had no intention of going to breakfast—or anywhere else, for that matter—with this pastor and his buddies. How could he get out of going now? He decided to decline outright.

"No," he said at last. "I don't want to go. Sorry."

Pastor Dave nodded. "I understand. No problem. Maybe in a couple of weeks … when we go to breakfast again." The man's dark eyes held Pete's, as if waiting for an answer.

He sighed. "Yeah. Well, maybe. We'll see."

The pastor's smile was warm. "Great! I'll check with you then. Meanwhile, how about a warm-up on these coffees? I could sure use one." He stood up and headed for the coffee pot.

"Okay. Thanks."

Now I've got to keep talking to him until we finish another cup of coffee. Pete glanced at his watch. Nearly one-thirty. Where were Rachel and Lilly? He sure wished they'd get home and rescue him so he could go back to his TV shows.

Thoughts ricocheted off one another, and he immediately wondered if the pastor's visit was coincidental with both Lilly and Rachel gone. They went to church together on

Sundays now, and Lilly had met with the pastor on more than one occasion. Were they all scheming against him? Sure seemed that way.

Rachel was exhausted, and she couldn't quite figure out why. She knew she'd had a wonderful lunch with Lilly, and she knew they'd driven quite a way to get to the restaurant. Was she really getting so old a pleasant outing with her daughter wore her out?

As she and Lilly made their way from the garage into the house, Rachel smiled at the sound of voices coming from the TV room. Seemed nothing had changed while they were gone. Pete still sat in the same chair, in the same room, watching the same shows. At times, the thought was depressing. Right now, for some reason, the thought warmed her heart.

"Hello, sweetheart," she said, as she entered the TV room, then bent down to kiss Pete's cheek. "Did you miss us?"

Pete hit the remote's mute button, then turned his head to look up at her. He shrugged. "I guess. Did you have a good time?"

"We did." Rachel sat in the rocker. "Did you know the fish place downtown, the one we used to go to all the time, is closed? I wanted so much to go there with Lilly, but we ended up going somewhere else instead."

Pete frowned. "The fish place closed years ago, Rachel. Don't you remember? You were upset even then. So nothing new has opened in its place?"

Rachel sighed. "Apparently not."

"So where'd you go instead?"

Pete's words caught her by surprise. Why had he asked her, and why didn't she know the answer?

"Hi, Dad." Lilly's entrance pushed the question from Rachel's mind. She smiled as she watched her daughter bend down to kiss her father's cheek.

"I was just asking your mother where you had lunch," Pete said, still looking up at his daughter. "I don't think she remembers."

Both Pete and Lilly's eyes turned toward her, and Rachel's face heated. She realized this was an answer she should know; but try as she might, she couldn't remember.

"We didn't eat at the fish place," she said, hoping Lilly would pick up the conversation from there. Thankfully, she did.

"No, we didn't," she said, smiling down at her mother. "The other place was closed, but we had a lovely time at the Sea Spray Inn over on the coast. The food was great, and we had a window seat overlooking the ocean. I really enjoyed it, didn't you, Mom?"

Relief rolled over Rachel, as she silently telegraphed a heartfelt thanks to her daughter for stepping in and helping her out, even though she still couldn't remember anything about the restaurant or being on the coast. "I truly did," she said, forcing a note of confidence into her voice. "I would love to go there again."

Lilly looked back down at her father as she placed her hand on his shoulder. "As would I." Her smile was warm. "But next time we want you to go with us, not for lunch but for dinner, so we can watch a sunset together. What do you think, Dad?"

A brief cloud shrouded his face, then quickly left. He shrugged. "I don't know. I don't really like to get out much, as you know. And besides, how often do we get to see the sunsets around here? We'd have to pick the perfect day."

"And we will." Lilly patted his shoulder. "We'll wait for that perfect day, without a cloud in the sky and then we'll drop our other plans and hop into the car. The coast is barely an hour's drive, so there's no reason we can't be spontaneous."

Lilly's and Pete's eyes locked, as if each waited on the other to speak. At last, Pete cleared his throat and broke the brief silence.

"Yeah, I guess." He turned his face back toward the TV, restoring the sound with the remote.

"So …" Lilly paused a moment, then asked, "So, nothing interesting happened while we were gone?"

Pete looked back up at her, not bothering to mute the TV this time. His scowl was accusatory. "Why? Were you expecting something to happen?"

Lilly ignored the question and smiled. "I'm going to make some tea. Anybody want to join me?"

Rachel rose from her chair. "That sounds wonderful, sweetheart. Thank you."

He'd been rude, mean even, when he didn't mute the TV to talk to Rachel or Lilly. But he'd already muted it once. He didn't see any reason to do so again, especially since his daughter's question had confirmed his suspicion—she'd set him up by sending the pastor to see him while she and her mother were gone.

I don't appreciate being blindsided, and I'll tell her so the next time I get her alone. Don't want to draw Rachel in. She has enough problems already.

He shook his head, scarcely hearing the afternoon news commentator opining on the latest scandal out of Washington. *Rachel really is getting bad—worse, actually. She's already been bad for a while now, but most of the time I can ignore her lapses. I don't think I can much longer. I'm glad Lilly's here to help me keep track of her mother.*

The thought gave him pause about confronting Lilly regarding sending the pastor to talk with him. *No sense alienating our daughter. I don't know how I'd handle things if she hadn't moved back home. I still wonder what we're going to do with Rachel when she completely loses her mind..*

Tears stung his eyes, and he quickly brushed them away. He wasn't about to let himself get emotional over something that couldn't be helped or fixed. But Rachel's condition sure was a growing worry—watching her slip away more often these days.

The pastor's earlier visit interrupted his thoughts. He was shocked to realize his heart yearned to talk to the man—or to anyone, for that matter, so long as he could talk to someone he could trust. Pete had kept so much inside for so long, and this wasn't good for him or anyone else around him. His anger and resentment had become such constant companions these past few years, he doubted there was a way to be free of them ever again. And in all honesty, he wasn't fully convinced he wanted to be.

He heard the two women's voices coming from the kitchen, no doubt laughing together as they drank their tea. His heart wrenched as he considered how many years had passed since he and Rachel had laughed together.

We were close once, Rachel. As close as any two people can be. We shared everything together. But now ...

Once again, he fought tears, as he forced his mind away from the wife he was losing, day by day, instead focusing his attention on the toothpaste commercial now filling the screen. *If life were as simple as picking the right toothpaste, I imagine I'd be a lot happier. No doubt my family would be too.*

Chapter 19

Lilly had forgotten how beautiful the church was at Christmastime. The huge tree at the front of the sanctuary, just to the right of the stage, was decorated from floor to ceiling and surrounded by large cardboard cutouts of those present at the manger scene where Jesus was born, drawing her glance every few minutes. And then there was the table to the left of the stage where the candles were lit, one each week leading up to Christmas, commemorating the Advent season.

Why have I stayed away for so long? I don't know if I'm ready to come back fulltime, but being here on the Sundays leading up to Christmas seems especially meaningful somehow.

As the service drew to a close, Lilly glanced sideways at her mother. Though still lovely for her age, Mom's face appeared older than even earlier this morning. Lilly shook her head. The thought made absolutely no sense, especially since her mother nearly glowed with joy as she sang the closing hymn.

Strange the way she goes in and out of reality. One minute she remembers every ingredient for one of her favorite recipes, even if she hasn't made it in years; the next, she can't remember what day it is or whether or not she's eaten. I know this is typical of the disease, but still …

The song came to a close, the pastor pronounced the benediction, and people began to pick up their belongings and head toward the back of the room. Mom and Lilly did the same, as the chatter level escalated around them.

I've seen a few people I knew when I came here as a child, but no one my own age. Lilly scanned the crowd, even as she kept close tabs on her mother. *That's too bad. I thought some of my old friends would still be around. Since they're not, I wonder if they've stopped coming to church, as I did. Or are they attending somewhere else? I really haven't made any attempts to reconnect with old friends here in Wildflower, and I'm just not sure I want to. At least not while I'm taking care of Mom. And once she's gone, then what? Do I continue to stay and take care of Dad? If not, do I even stay in town, or go elsewhere? My writing job, at least for now, goes anywhere I do. At some point, however, I'm going to want something more substantial, more permanent—*

Her mother laid her hand on Lilly's arm, interrupting her thoughts. Mom's eyes registered something akin to panic. "I need to use the restroom before we leave," she whispered, leaning close so her daughter could hear. "But I can't remember where it is."

Lilly's heart ached at what her mother must be feeling, but she did her best not to react. No sense adding to her mom's distress.

"I'll walk you over," she said, smiling to give encouragement. "Then I'll wait for you until you come out."

Her mother's forehead relaxed, as she held on to her daughter's arm while they walked. "I'll be right out here," Lilly said, then her mother went inside.

While she waited, Lilly watched the remaining parishioners milling around, some standing in groups or pairs, chatting, and a few sharing brief words of prayer together. *I was such a part of this at one time. How did I let myself drift so far away?*

Before she could search for an answer, she spotted Pastor Dave, smiling as he approached. He was obviously heading her way, so she returned the smile.

"Waiting for your mom?" he asked.

"Yes. She wanted to make a quick stop before we head home."

"Sounds like my wife. We live in the parsonage half a block away, but she still insists on stopping in here before we go home." He chuckled. "So," he said, as if he were changing the subject, "has your dad said anything about my visit?"

Lilly felt her eyes go wide. So Pastor Dave had gone to visit her dad after all. "I didn't even know you'd been there," she said, "so obviously not. Dad didn't say a word."

"Ah. Well, I'm not too surprised. He didn't exactly welcome me with open arms—which I certainly didn't expect him to—but he didn't completely rebuff me either. In fact, he made a pot of coffee, which we shared in the kitchen while we had a brief talk."

Lilly was stunned. "He made a pot of coffee?" She shook her head. "I can't remember the last time he did anything domestic. If Mom or I don't make his coffee—or food, or anything else for that matter—he does without and sure lets us know."

They both chuckled this time. "Yes, I thought that might be the way it is," Pastor Dave said. "I actually felt quite privileged to be invited in at all, and then to share coffee with him ... Well, overall, I'd say it was a good first visit."

"A first visit? Do you intend to see him again?"

"Absolutely. Sometime this week or next, I plan to go by and invite him to join some of the men for breakfast. We go out to eat every other Saturday morning, before heading out into the community to help fix yards, do a little repair work ... you know, for the elderly or single moms. Just a small way to extend Christ's love beyond the doors of our church. We help anyone in our congregation who is in need, but we also offer help to those who don't attend our church."

"Interesting." Lilly was impressed. "I like that idea. So you told my dad about the ministry and invited him to come? Surely he didn't accept, did he?"

Dave smiled and shook his head. "No, not really. At least not for yesterday. But he did leave the door open for the next time we get together—two weeks from yesterday, to be exact. I told him I'd be in touch and would be happy to pick him up and bring him to breakfast with us. He can decide if he wants to come along on our work projects. If not, I'll bring him home after we eat."

"Wow. The fact he invited you in and made coffee is surprising enough, but that he didn't throw you out with an absolutely 'no, never' is beyond astonishing. I'm actually quite impressed."

"Well, his joining us isn't a done deal yet, so keep praying, will you? I haven't stopped since I saw him, and I won't quit now. In fact, I believe your Dad's being receptive at all was God's answer to prayer."

Could be. "Maybe, but he hasn't accepted your invitation yet."

"Exactly why we need to pray. There's nothing too hard for God, you know."

She spoke the words she'd memorized as a child, surprised she still recalled the Scripture. "'With God, nothing is impossible,'"

"Exactly."

Lilly was beginning to feel a bit more comfortable in the support group, especially as she listened to the stories others told about their own journeys of walking a loved one through what often seemed the unfathomable maze of Alzheimer's. Many in the group, like Lilly, were caring for an elderly parent, while others cared for a spouse. Each had their own set of difficulties.

"By the time I finally get my mother into bed at night," one attendee named Karen said, "I am so exhausted, I can scarcely stay on my feet long enough to collapse into my own bed. But I think the loneliness bothers me most. I know my mom and I are living in the same house, but she hardly recognizes me anymore. Sometimes I feel as if my mom is already gone, and I'm taking care of a stranger all alone" She shook her head as she looked around the group. Tears shone in her pale blue eyes as she spoke again. "If it weren't for all of you, I don't know what I'd do."

Those nearest to Karen reached out and patted her arm or squeezed her hand. One group member crossed the circle to hand her a tissue.

A small gesture but appreciated.

"My problem is a bit different," ventured a man whose nametag read *Ken.* "My dad has Alzheimer's, as most of you know, and lives with my wife, Margaret, and me. Lately, I see the toll all this is taking on my wife—not to mention on our marriage. During nearly all of my dad's waking hours, either Margaret or I have to be with him, doing everything for him and being especially careful he doesn't wander off." Ken shook his head. "Unfortunately, he somehow figured out how to get out of the house yesterday, wearing nothing but his underwear. When we found him—which, thankfully, was just moments after he escaped—he told us he was going shopping for some clothes. 'Just look at me,' he kept saying, as we led him back to the house. 'It's a disgrace this is all I have to wear.' We showed him his closet, which is full of clothes, and even opened every drawer in his dresser. But he was still adamant he had no clothes. My poor wife seems at the end of her rope. I'm not much help to her because by the end of the day, neither of us has any energy or strength left to spend anything close to quality time together."

Lilly counted her blessings because her mother hadn't done anything like what Ken described ... yet. Still, there were no guarantees similar incidents wouldn't transpire in the near future.

Lena, the group leader, stepped in, her question direct but compassionate. "Is your dad still talking about not having any clothes?"

Ken sighed. "We were so sure he'd forget, but the first thing out of his mouth this morning was that he wanted to go shopping for some clothes."

Lena offered an understanding smile. "Have you considered taking him on a brief shopping trip—just enough to buy him a new shirt and a pair of pants?"

Ken looked doubtful. "We haven't taken him much of anywhere lately, at least not since he's been this bad." He paused, as if mulling over the suggestion. "Do you think taking him to a store would help?"

Lena shrugged. "No guarantees, as you well know. But as long as you and Margaret plan the trip carefully, it just might."

"I suppose we could take him in the wheelchair. Though he can still walk on his own, I don't think he's physically strong enough to pull himself out of the wheelchair without at least some help. With both Margaret and me watching over him, we shouldn't have any worries about him getting away from us."

Some of the others in the group encouraged Ken to take his father shopping. Before long, the man looked a bit more encouraged.

"One other thing," Lena said. "Have you asked Margaret to join us here? You're both care-partners for your dad, and I'm sure she'd feel better if she could share her feelings with the group. Is that a possibility, Ken?"

He shrugged. "I suppose. I've asked her a couple times before, but she declined. I haven't asked in a while, though. And things with Dad have gotten worse since then, so she might be more open now. The problem is, who will take care of Dad while we're gone?"

"Remind me to give you a couple of numbers after we dismiss tonight," Lena said. "I think we can find someone to come in for a couple hours one evening a week. Then maybe you and your wife could stop for a quick dinner on your way to group. This might just give you some together-time you've been missing."

Lilly was pleasantly surprised at how the group pulled together to support and encourage one another. So far, she hadn't shared much beyond the basics of her own situation, but maybe next week she would. Her problems seemed almost trivial compared to what some had shared, but her mother's condition would no doubt continue to worsen with time. Still, she couldn't imagine chasing after her mom as she hurried down the street in her underwear, ready to go on a shopping spree.

If not for being so sad, I'd be laughing at the thought.

"You go to that group thing again?"

Dad's question caught Lilly off-guard. They sat at the kitchen table, their breakfast of fruit and bagels finished. Mom had headed off to the shower, leaving the two of them to enjoy a final cup of coffee together.

Lilly tried to read her father's expression, but his eyes were focused on his cup.

"Yes, I did," she said. "And I believe I'll continue to attend weekly. Did I tell you they meet every Thursday evening at a church downtown?" Not waiting for an answer, she took a deep breath and forged ahead. "You could come too, you know. We could get someone to stay with Mom for a couple of hours, and we could go together."

She waited while her father squeezed his coffee cup with both hands. She knew he was trying to control his response, which wasn't always something he did well.

"Not going to happen," he said, slowly raising his head to lock his eyes onto hers. "You can go all you want—I'll stay here with your mother. But I'm not about to go to some meeting and talk about how crazy my wife is."

Lilly resisted the impulse to lay her hand on her dad's arm. "Mom's not crazy, Dad. She has a disease affecting her memory, that's all."

Dad harrumphed. "Well, crazy or not, I'm not going to talk about her in front of a bunch of people I don't even know."

"I had a lot of reservations when I first went too," she said, keeping her voice calm and even. "But after being there only a few times, I feel as if I know those people— as if we're connected somehow." This time she followed through with her impulse and laid her hand on her dad's arm. He flinched but didn't draw away. "They're all dealing with similar problems, Dad. They're all care-partners with someone who has Alzheimer's."

Dad scowled. "Care-partners? What's that supposed to mean?"

Lilly took another deep breath. "Care-partners is a term the group likes to use, rather than caregivers. They believe the term helps keep their situation in perspective. We're reminded we're working *with* our loved one, in a partnership, rather than strictly *for* them, reducing them to victims and increasing the chance we might begin to think of ourselves as martyrs. It's a way to help reduce the likelihood of building resentment toward our loved one with the disease."

"Are you trying to tell me something as simple as changing a word keeps you from getting resentful? I find that a little hard to believe."

"Of course not." Lilly once again resisted an impulse— this time to remind him resentment can build from our own selfish choices. "But anything to help get us through something as tough as this is a good thing, right?" When her father didn't respond, she added, "So will you come with me sometime?"

Again, Dad shook his head, this time more adamantly. "Not a chance. So don't bother to ask again."

Lilly sighed and withdrew her hand. The conversation was over, so she might as well wash the breakfast dishes.

Chapter 20

The TV blared his usual game show, but Pete scarcely heard a word. Try as he might, he couldn't stop thinking of his conversation with Lilly. He tried to picture himself sitting in a group of people, all talking about how miserable their lives had become because someone they cared about was losing their mind.

Because that's the truth of the matter. Whether Lilly wants to admit it or not, whether she wants to call it a disease or a condition or whatever, my wife is losing her mind. At least she still knows me now, but for how much longer?

He shook his head, trying to ignore the tears prickling his eyelids. He couldn't afford to get emotional about the situation. True, Lilly was here to take care of her mother, but what about after? What if he outlived Rachel? Would Lilly stay on to take care of him too?

Ringing bells and squeals of excitement pierced his thoughts. He turned his attention to the TV long enough to realize a woman with bright orange hair had just won a prize. Now she had to decide whether to keep what she'd won or give it up for a chance to win something bigger and better. *Idiot. Are you really going to risk something good in hopes of getting something better? Haven't you lived long enough to figure out if you make a bet like that you'll lose everything?*

The woman seemed caught in a dilemma, as she looked from the prize she'd already won to the large game board showing the prize she could win.

Or not, Pete thought.

The woman with the orange hair threw her hands into the air and began to jump up and down. "I'm going for it!" she screamed, and the live audience began to holler and applaud with her.

Pete muted the sound. He already knew how her gamble would turn out.

Once again, he let his mind drift back to the imaginary support group he'd been thinking about earlier. *More fools. Just like the woman with the orange hair. Everybody risking what already is, in hopes of getting something that might be ... but most likely isn't. When will they learn?*

Pete decided he wasn't about to become like them. He knew he could no longer depend on Rachel to do everything for him. At least for now, there was Lilly; and she did a better job with the meals than her mother had been doing lately. So he'd stay home from support groups—and anywhere else he didn't want to go—and deal with life as it truly was, not as he wished it might be.

He sighed and his shoulders sagged, as a pang of guilt stabbed his heart. *This is about more than Rachel not being able to take care of me anymore, isn't it? This is also about me, pitching in to help Lilly take care of her mother—my wife.*

The *care-partner* term floated into his thoughts then, and with it, tears that would not be stopped. *What am I going to do? How can I help? I can't even walk on my own.*

From deep inside, he heard the answer: *I will carry you.*

He realized he'd been praying—and he'd just heard the answer.

Is that you, God? If it is, tell me what to do. How do I deal with this? What's going on?

The doorbell pulled his attention back from his jumbled thoughts and emotions. Scarcely wondering who might be at the door, he raised his head just in time to see the orange-haired woman, once again jumping up and down and screaming, as she saw her gamble pay off. She'd won the bigger prize.

✦✳✧✦

Minutes later, Pete quickly brushed away his tears when he heard his daughter's voice.

"Look who's here," Lilly said, as she stood in the doorway, ushering their guest into the TV room. "Pastor Dave came to see you, Dad."

She looked at the pastor. "Can I offer you something to drink? Coffee or tea or ...?"

Pastor Dave shook his head. "No, thanks. I can't stay long. I just wanted to check in with your dad about something we discussed before."

Pete tensed, as he wondered what was coming, though he had a pretty good idea.

"How are you, Pete?" the pastor asked, stretching out his hand.

"Fine." Pete reached up to shake the pastor's hand while watching him warily.

He glanced at the seat next to Pete's. "Mind if I sit down? I'll only be a few minutes."

"Sure. Go ahead."

Pastor Dave smiled and sat down in the rocker. "I'm sorry I didn't come by sooner. I meant to, but the past few days got away from me."

Pete considered asking why the pastor hadn't just called but decided instead to sit and wait to hear what was on his mind.

"Anyway, I imagine you remember what we discussed when I was here a couple weeks ago."

Pete held his tongue. Of course he remembered what they'd talked about, but he wasn't about to be the first one to verbalize it. He was having enough trouble trying to decide how he would respond when the pastor actually asked.

After a brief pause, Dave tried again. "About the men's breakfast and work day ... remember? I know you said you didn't think you'd want to join us for the work part, but the invitation to come and have breakfast with us is still open—as is my offer of a ride. I can pick you up tomorrow morning, just before eight." Pastor Dave smiled again. "So what do you think, Pete? Is it a date?"

Pete readied to decline the invitation, but the words wouldn't come. Instead, he heard the silent voice again: *Let me carry you, Pete.*

Quickly swallowing the lump in his throat, he found himself nodding. "Sure," he said, amazed his voice worked. "I'll give it a try. Just this once, though."

Pastor Dave's smile nearly split his face, as he grabbed Pete's right hand, then clapped him on the shoulder. "This is wonderful! I can't tell you how pleased I am you accepted. I'm already looking forward to our time together tomorrow. And I know the other men will feel exactly the same way."

Pete wasn't sure he believed the other men in the group would welcome him, but he'd find out soon enough. He just hoped he wasn't making another doozy of a mistake. He knew better than anyone how many of those he'd already made in his lifetime, and the thought was just about enough for him to change his mind about the breakfast plans.

Then again, he had heard a voice—God's?

What was I thinking? Why did I let myself get talked into this?

Pete sat in the front passenger seat of Pastor Dave's car, waiting for him to retrieve Pete's walker from the trunk. *I could be home in my comfortable chair, watching one of my regular shows and drinking another cup of coffee. Instead, I'm about to go into a restaurant to eat breakfast with a bunch of guys I don't even know. I just hope breakfast doesn't turn into some sort of hallelujah-shouting match.*

Pastor Dave opened Pete's door and set up his walker so he could swing his legs around in order to reach his walker. With no other real options, that's exactly what he did.

The other men greeted Pete as soon as he walked into the restaurant. In moments, he sat at a fairly large, rear round table, perusing a menu and wondering what to order. The waitress had already brought water and coffee.

They seem welcoming enough, but I can't help but wonder what they think of me being on a walker. They probably know I can't pitch in to help with the work they're going to do after we eat. And then there's the bigger question: What do they think about me not going to church? I guess they must think I'm some kind of heathen or something.

"I'll take the pancake special."

The voice of the man across from him—whose name Pete had already forgotten—caught his attention. He looked up from his menu to see the waitress beginning to take their orders.

He looked back at the menu but still couldn't decide. When the waitress stopped next to him, her pen poised above her order pad, he ordered the only thing that came to mind. "I'll take the pancake special too."

She jotted his order down, then asked how he'd like his eggs. *Served at home.* "Over easy," he said and breathed a sigh of relief as she moved on to the next person.

With orders given and their coffee and waters in place—plus orange juice for two of the men—the group was now free to talk among themselves. Pete was relieved they were at the very back of the restaurant. People might still hear them if they got loud, but at least there was a chance they wouldn't draw too much attention.

"So, Pete," the guy on his right said, "do you still work, or are you retired?"

Pete glanced at his walker, folded up now and leaning against the wall behind Pastor Dave. *Do I look like I'm still working?* He considered explaining he'd had to take an early retirement after the accident, and how he received only partial disability, but thought better of verbalizing his situation. *Why give them any more information than necessary? It's not like they actually care.*

"I'm retired," he said, hoping no one asked the next obvious question: *What did you do before retiring?* But of course, someone did, and the conversation continued, with him at the center. Thankfully, Pastor Dave jumped in and changed the subject.

"Our food should be here any minute," he said. "Why don't we go ahead and pray now so we can eat when it arrives? Jim, would you lead us in prayer this morning?"

The man named Jim bowed his head, and everyone else—including Pete—did the same. He was relieved when the prayer didn't go on too long, and afterward the discussion centered on the pros and cons of beginning a second Sunday service. Since Pete knew nothing about the topic, he felt exonerated for not saying anything.

By the time the food arrived, everyone dug right in. Pete tried to do the same, but the eggs were overdone and the bacon not crisp enough. He tried the pancakes and decided they tasted pretty good, even if they were too heavy. All in all, breakfast wasn't nearly as good as it would have been at home.

Soon, the waitress had presented their checks. The men dug into their wallets, then tossed money into a pile in the middle of the table. Pete reached into his own pocket to do the same, but Pastor Dave stopped him.

"This one's on me," he said, smiling broadly. "You're our guest this time. After today, you can buy your own."

Everyone chuckled, and Pete thanked him, though he would have preferred to pay his own way. *I don't like being beholden to anyone. But then, I won't be coming back after today, so it won't really matter.*

The man named Jim picked up all the money from the center of the table and went to the front of the restaurant to pay. Pastor Dave grabbed Pete's walker, opened it, and set it in front of him. Relieved, Pete hoisted himself up and proceeded to the front door with the rest of their group.

Chapter 21

The mall was decorated in all the bright colors of the season, but Rachel couldn't find one mention of Christmas. Confusing. Certainly Christmas was nearly upon them. Why else would Lilly be home from school?

Why not simply ask? "Lilly"—Rachel lay her hand on her daughter's arm—"isn't it almost Christmas?"

Lilly slowed her pace, then turned and smiled. "Yes. Almost. In a few weeks."

Rachel hesitated before continuing. "Then why aren't there any *Merry Christmas* signs somewhere here in the mall? I've been looking for something that mentions Christmas but can only find bright colors, as if they were decorating for some generic holiday. I don't even see a Christmas tree."

Lilly stopped walking altogether. "I'm afraid you're right, Mom. Christmas has nearly become a generic holiday now because that's all we can celebrate publicly— an effort not to leave anyone out ... you know, those who don't share our faith."

Rachel frowned. "Well, that doesn't make sense. Ever since I was a child. I've known people who weren't Christians, and yet they still celebrated Christmas. The Santa-and-presents part of it, I'll admit, but ..."

Lilly's face brightened. "You just reminded me of something." She took her mother's arm and steered her toward the other end of the mall.

"Where are we going?" Rachel asked.

Lilly's face was still glowing. "You'll see."

Before long, Rachel spotted a long line of children and adults—parents, no doubt—snaking down one side of the mall. As soon as she could see the beginning of the line, she knew exactly where Lilly was taking her.

"Santa!" Rachel clapped her hands, feeling youthful once again. "So, even though it's only the commercial side of Christmas, Santa hasn't been abolished entirely."

Lilly smiled. "Exactly. And, look! There's an empty bench over there. Let's sit down and watch. What do you say?"

Delighted, Rachel sat down beside her daughter and watched the scene unfold in front of them. Children— some nearly teenagers, others still babies and toddlers— had their moment on Santa's lap. Many of the youngest children seemed none too eager to sit on the stranger's lap while doting parents managed to get the desired pictures, even if the children's mouths were open, screaming. As far as Santa, little had changed since Lilly—or Rachel, herself, for that matter—was a child. Rachel remembered how Lilly squirmed and howled, trying to escape the jolly man with the white beard. After all these years, Rachel still had the picture displayed on her refrigerator.

"Where has the time gone?" she wondered aloud.

Lilly took her mother's hand. "Flown by, that's for sure."

Rachel nodded, a bittersweet longing tugging at her heart. She knew she was coming close to the end of her earthly life, which in many ways thrilled her. But she was also saddened to know she would soon leave Pete and Lilly behind.

Or would she? What if Pete went first? Did he know the Lord? The answer loomed dark in her thoughts; but with God, there was always the light of hope.

And Lilly? True, she had stopped going to church in her teens. But now she was home from college and accompanying Rachel most every Sunday. This brought Rachel peace. Knowing her family would still be intact after her death made all the difference. She would have to double her prayer time with this focus in mind.

She sighed. There seemed to be so much happening lately, things Rachel couldn't understand or remember. But as to her relationship with the Lord, she believed her faith was growing stronger with each passing day. Talking with her Father was the one time she knew her mind was clear, and he was there with her.

"Thank you," she whispered.

"Did you say something, Mom?"

Rachel blinked and turned to look at Lilly, then smiled. "No, I don't think so, sweetheart. Let's go find you something special for Christmas. Shopping together will be like when you were a little girl. I used to bring you here to this very mall, you know."

Lilly squeezed her mother's hand. "I remember. And the time we spent together was nearly as special then as it is now." She squeezed Rachel's hand. "So, let's get going. How about starting with our favorite store?"

Rachel's heart soared, not only because of her daughter's suggestion, but also because she knew exactly which store Lilly meant. Rachel considered everything she could remember, no matter how seemingly insignificant to anyone else, a victory.

They rose from the bench and, arm-in-arm, headed off to do some shopping.

Thursday night had rolled around again, and Lilly sat in a circle with the rest of the group. They would meet one more time before Christmas and then take a break until after the New Year.

When Lena reminded the group about the break, one woman spoke up. "What if ...?" She seemed to swallow a sob. "What if we need to talk to someone during the break? I can't tell you how many times throughout the week things happen that make me count the days—and even the hours—until the next group meeting. I know we'll only miss two meetings, but the holidays can be an especially stressful time. I'm worried about getting through them without someone to talk to—someone who understands."

Lena leaned forward. "You never have to go this alone," she said, her voice and words warm and reassuring. "How many of you would feel better knowing you had someone to call and talk with during those two weeks when we're not meeting?"

Every hand went up, including Lilly's. She too had found herself looking forward to the next support group meeting and had been a bit concerned about those two weeks in between.

The leader clapped her hands together. "It's unanimous. Okay, here's what I suggest, though if you care to manage some other way, this would be fine too. I'll put a signup sheet on the table by the door. When you leave tonight, write your name and phone number on the list. If you have someone in the group you'd especially like to partner with, then don't sign up; you can connect on your own. For everyone else, I'll go through the list and assign each of you a partner, then call you with the information. This will be the person you contact when you really need to connect with someone you know will understand. When we return after the first of the year, you can disband your partnerships ... or not. I'll leave that entirely to each of you to decide."

Lilly thought the idea was a good one and resolved to put her name and cellphone number on the list. Her mind settled, she listened as the group began discussion and sharing time.

"I heard there was some new treatment for Alzheimer's," said a woman named Joan. "It has something to do with stem cells, I think."

Lena nodded. "I've heard the same thing. I need to see what I can find out about it. If anyone else knows more, please fill us in."

Lilly felt deflated. For a brief moment, she'd felt hopeful, as she imagined everyone else had as well. No doubt someone would one day come up with a cure for this dreadful, mind-stealing disease. Until then, they would simply have to walk through this valley as best they could.

Help us, Lord. Lilly blinked as she realized what she'd done. *This is becoming a bad habit.* She swallowed a chuckle. *Maybe a good one.*

✱❋✿✧

Pete sat at the table, sipping coffee and waiting for Lilly to finish scrambling the eggs. He glared at his wife, wondering what Rachel was up to now.

"I'm going out to buy a Christmas tree," she announced, her purse slung over her shoulder and her winter coat buttoned tight, as she stood in the kitchen doorway. "Does anyone want to come with me?"

"Are you crazy?" he asked. "You know you can't drive anymore."

A flash of pain crossed Rachel's face, and Pete knew the fault was his. He was tired of tiptoeing around what needed to be said. Better she feel a little pain than go wandering on the roads.

Lilly came up beside Pete and laid her hand on his shoulder, then turned to talk to her mother. "That's all right, Mom. I think getting a Christmas tree is a great idea. Why not sit down and have breakfast first? The eggs are almost ready. Then I'll take you, I promise." She squeezed

Pete's shoulder. "Maybe we can all go. After all, you and Dad have always picked out our trees together."

Rachel's face lit up. "That's a wonderful idea!" She stepped over to the kitchen table, where she removed her coat and laid it and her purse on an empty chair. "Picking out the tree together will be just like old times," she said, leaning down to kiss Pete's cheek. "Maybe we can even stop for lunch somewhere. Won't that be fun?"

Now, why'd she have to go and mention lunch? First, Lilly suggests something she knows I don't want to do, and then Rachel jumps in and starts making plans to go out and eat. He sighed. *Then she had to go and seal the idea with a kiss. Looks like I'm stuck, whether I want to go or not.*

"Fine," he said, grabbing his coffee mug and taking another swig. He looked up at Lilly. "Any chance I can get a refill? This one's cold."

Before Lilly could answer, Rachel took his cup and carried it over to the sink. "I'll get it for you, sweetheart."

Lilly still stood at his side, but now a grin had spread across her face. If he didn't know better, he'd think they cooked this up together.

Well, there goes my morning TV. He smiled in spite of himself. *I wonder what else those two have been plotting against me.*

Lilly gave his shoulder a final squeeze, then walked back to the stove, just as Rachel returned to the table with two full cups in hand. Setting one in front of Pete, she settled down with the second cup in the seat next to him. In minutes, they were all eating scrambled eggs and toast, as Rachel and Lilly rambled on about Christmas trees and where they wanted to eat lunch. When they asked Pete's opinion, he shrugged and said he didn't care.

Which is true, since I don't want to go anyway, but I obviously don't have a choice.

As he ate, he listened to his wife's words. Her mind seemed especially clear this morning. *How does this work? One day she seems to know nearly everything that's going on—and the next she can't remember what year it is, let alone what month or day.* He shook his head and took another bite of toast. What bothered him most was that even on her best days, Rachel seemed unable to get past Lilly's years in college. You'd think she'd at least remember working with Jacob and then introducing him to Lilly, especially since Rachel had made such a huge deal about Lilly's wedding.

He drained his coffee cup for the second time, resolving not to have a third. He had no idea how long the three of them would be on their outing and he hated using public restrooms, especially since he was on a walker.

His mind returned to his daughter's wedding. *I don't know if I've ever seen Rachel so happy, not even at our own wedding. When Lilly and Jacob split up, Rachel cried for days. I wonder if this is why she's stuck on thinking of Lilly as still being in college.*

"Dad?"

Lilly's voice cut into his thoughts, and he looked up from his nearly empty plate.

"Can I get you anything else?" she asked.

Pete shook his head. "No. I'm full. Thanks."

Rachel patted Pete's hand. "Besides," she said, "we need to save room for lunch, right?"

Pete turned his gaze from his daughter to his wife. Rachel's soft brown eyes sparkled as he'd seldom seen them do lately, warming his heart. Obviously, she was excited about their plans, even though they were plans he wished they'd carry out without him. Why couldn't she forget about their tree-buying-and-lunch trip, like she did everything else?

He nearly chuckled. Rachel wasn't about to forget, so he might as well make the best of it. "I guess so," he said.

Rachel leaned over and once again kissed him on the cheek. She sure knew how to get to him.

Chapter 22

The weather was cooperating quite nicely, offering the threesome a sunny, if brisk, morning. The weather added to the fun of tree-shopping, even if this was their third tree lot. Lilly smiled as she watched her parents bicker back and forth about a tree being too tall, too sparse on one side, or not green enough.

Lilly chuckled, reminded of how they'd behaved the exact same way when she was a child. Sooner or later, though, they'd find that perfect tree and then the setting-up-and-decorating process would begin in earnest. Her mom had especially adored Christmas, decorating every nook and cranny of the house and baking almost daily in the run-up to Christmas Eve.

Christmas Eve. Unbidden, she recalled the first Christmas Eve she'd spent with Jacob. They'd been married only a few months, but that was the night she realized she and her new husband would most likely never share this tradition—one so precious to her.

Not that I had a right to expect anything else. Jacob is Jewish, even if only nominally. He'd told me almost from day one he didn't plan to observe any religious holidays, Christmas included. I had no idea how much I'd miss the fun, especially since I'd stopped attending church years before I met Jacob. Something about Christmas ... to not celebrate this holiday ...

In all fairness, Jacob had encouraged her to spend Christmas with her parents so she could celebrate as she wished, though he himself didn't care to be involved. After wrestling with her emotions, she decided spending the holiday with her husband was more important, even if they weren't celebrating in any visible way.

Lilly pushed her thoughts aside and stepped from one row of trees to the next, following behind her parents and letting them set the pace. Dad had been resistant at first, insisting he would wait in the car while Lilly and her mother got the tree; but she and her mother refused to let him.

"We're all three going to celebrate Christmas together this year," Lilly said, "for the first time in quite a while, so this means you have to be involved in all the planning and preparation. Come on, Dad. It'll be like old times."

Lilly had known, even then, her words were a bit of an exaggeration, as her mother could drift off at any point and completely forget what they were doing. But Lilly had stood her ground, and firmness had worked. Dad got out of the car and pushed his walker around as best he could, stopping to check out each tree Mom seemed to favor. They'd seen quite a few by now, and Lilly wondered how long before they would come to an agreement over one particular tree.

"Here it is!" Mom's high-pitched voice rang out with excitement and conviction. "The perfect tree! Pete, come and look. Isn't it perfect?"

Dad joined Mom in their closer inspection of the Douglas Fir. It was just under six feet, full and even on all sides. Her mother might just be right about this one.

"I like it," Dad said, his first positive words about any of the trees they'd seen so far.

Lilly felt a temporary rush of relief. Even as she watched Dad barter with the man selling the trees, she realized they'd have to tie the tree to the roof—not too much of a problem, since they were only a couple miles from home. But what about lunch? She supposed they could drop off the tree at home and then go to lunch, but she didn't want to risk losing her dad to the lure of his TV room or her mom to her canyon of nostalgic memories.

As Dad pulled his wallet from his pocket and counted out the bills, Lilly decided they would take the tree, on top of the car, to lunch with them. And she knew just the place.

✳ ❋ ✧ ✧

Pete realized he shouldn't have given in, should have insisted on taking the tree straight home and having lunch there. But Rachel and Lilly had nearly begged him to follow through on their lunch plans.

"You and Mom haven't been out to eat together in far too long," Lilly had insisted. "Besides, I'm taking you to a very special place, something that just opened in the past couple of months, so I'm sure neither of you have been there yet. I've eaten there only once, just a few days ago. I discovered the place by accident, but I really like it. The food is good—reasonable too—and we can sit outside in the sunshine where we can keep an eye on the car."

"And on our tree," Rachel added, her face hopeful.

Our tree. When she'd said those words, Pete's memory flashed back to their first married Christmas together and how much fun they'd had picking out a tree that would actually fit in their tiny studio apartment. *Our tree.* Rachel had referred to the tree with those exact words from the moment she'd laid eyes on it, declaring it perfect, much as she'd done today. The memory of the beautiful young woman he'd married and how deeply he'd loved her, nearly from the moment he'd first laid eyes on her, tugged at his heart until there was no fight left in him.

"Fine," he'd said, then turned his attention to the man who now held Pete's money. "Can you tie it to the top of the car for us?" He glanced down at his walker, then back up. "As you can see, I wouldn't be able to do it."

Pete didn't give the ladies time to offer. "I brought an old blanket with us, one we've used to help us get trees home for years, so all you'll have to do is hoist the tree onto the car roof and help us tie it down." He smiled at the man. "We sure do thank you for helping."

And now the three of them were headed down the road, tree safely tied down above them, when Lilly said, "That was nice of that man to help us with the tree."

"It's part of his job," Pete said. "And if not, then helping should be. Happy customers are the best advertising for any business."

When Rachel, seated in the front passenger seat, turned around to look at him, Pete found himself once again noticing the softness of her brown eyes. His wife might be sixty-seven, but she was still a looker.

"I was proud of you back there, Pete. You handled everything perfectly."

Pete's heart swelled. He couldn't remember when Rachel had last complimented him so sincerely. He blinked back tears and nodded. "Thanks," was all he could manage to say.

Lilly flipped on her blinker and followed up with a right turn before pulling into a large dirt parking lot. Several other cars were already parked in a row on one side of the lot, directly in front of a small eatery. When they parked and got out of the car, Pete could see people sitting at tables inside, next to the windows. Only a brave few sat outside in the tepid winter sunshine.

"All right, you two," Lilly said as she held the door open to let her parents go in first, "you get to make the choice. Do you want to eat inside where it's warm or outside where it's cooler but lovely?"

Pete waited to see how Rachel would answer. If they were still young, he knew she'd opt for an outside seat, cold or not. They were far from young anymore. If she preferred sitting inside, this would be fine.

Rachel stopped directly in front of him and looked up into his face. "Let's eat outside," she suggested, her eyes dancing with excitement. "We can eat inside anytime. Let's do something different."

Pete returned her smile. "If that's what you want, then that's what we'll do." He wished he could let go of his walker and pull her into his arms. The thought nearly knocked him from his feet, and he quickly dismissed the notion.

Lilly smiled at both of them, then turned to the waitress who was about to seat them. "We'll eat outside," she said. The young woman, whose long blonde ponytail swayed from side to side as she walked, led them out into the winter sunshine.

Pete was amazed at how well Rachel had done while they were out. Not only did she find the "perfect tree," but she handled herself quite nicely at lunch.

And then they got home.

He sighed. How quickly she could change! Sane and rational one minute, and then ...

"But we have to decorate the tree right now," she argued with Lilly. "It's almost Christmas!"

Obviously, Lilly was doing her best to be patient with her mother. "Yes, Christmas is almost here, but we can wait a couple of hours to decorate the tree. We can all get a good rest first and then we'll feel more like decorating."

Rachel stomped her foot. "But I feel like decorating right now. And besides, it's the next thing. We have to do the next thing!"

Pete stood in amazement, leaning on his walker and watching the scene play out in the entryway. They'd scarcely gotten inside the house before Rachel began making her demands, and Pete wondered what was next.

Should he step in and try to help Lilly soothe her mother? Rachel had always been so calm, so reasonable, so easy to talk with ... until now.

"Mom," Lilly said, her voice soft but firm as she took her mother's hands in hers and gazed into her eyes, "I know you want to decorate right now, but a couple of hours won't make any difference ... except we'll all feel more like doing it then. I'll even make some hot cider to drink while we're decorating. What do you think?"

Pete held his breath, as he waited to see if Rachel would give in. Instead, she shook off her daughter's hands and burst into tears. "You're all against me!" she screamed. "You don't love me anymore. You talk about me behind my back and hide my things. If you don't stop, I'm going to call the police!"

Pete couldn't stay put another minute. Moving his walker quickly toward the two women, he used his softest, most convincing voice. "Rachel," he said, "sweetheart, listen to me, please. Lilly and I love you more than you can imagine. We wouldn't intentionally do anything to hurt you. But if we did somehow, we are really sorry. We'll try harder, won't we, Lilly?"

He glanced at his daughter, whose eyes were wide, no doubt in surprise at his intervention. She nodded, and Pete turned back to Rachel.

"You see? Lilly agrees with me. So please, sweetheart, come with me. We'll both go to the bedroom and lie down for a while. You don't have to sleep if you don't want to. We can just rest for an hour or so, and then Lilly will make us hot cider. We can drink it while we decorate the beautiful tree you picked out."

Rachel's brown eyes flashed with emotion, but Pete held his ground. He wasn't sure where he'd gotten the words he spoke to her, but he somehow knew they were the right ones.

At last Rachel sighed, and Pete saw the anger abate as she relaxed. "Okay," she said, her voice soft and gentle now, the way Pete was used to hearing her. "Maybe that's a good idea. I am a bit tired."

She took off her coat and scarf and handed them and her purse to Lilly, then turned to follow Pete down the hallway. Pete held his peace, not wanting to say anything to trigger a mood swing. Apparently Lilly felt the same way, as she hadn't said a word since Rachel agreed to rest a while before tackling the tree.

They'd gone only a few steps when Rachel turned back toward Lilly. "I'll do this on one condition," she said, her voice sweet but firm. "We have to bake something while we decorate and drink hot cider. I love to smell Christmas goodies baking while I decorate."

Lilly's expression quickly changed from surprise to compliance. "Sure, Mom," she said. "That sounds like a great idea. While you and Dad rest, I'll see what ingredients we have in the kitchen. Then we can put something together and get it into the oven before we start on the tree."

Seemingly satisfied, Rachel turned back to Pete. "Lead on," she said, smiling as if she'd won a great victory. Pete, on the other hand, couldn't decide if he wanted to laugh or cry. Wisely, he did neither.

Chapter 23

Lilly rummaged through the kitchen cupboards, pulling out flour and sugar and cinnamon, marveling at the scene she'd just witnessed. Her mother's behavior, though difficult, wasn't so surprising or even new and would no doubt happen again. No, Lilly had not been surprised at her mother's behavior—she had found her father's response to her mother to be very surprising.

I can't remember the last time Dad stood up and took his responsibility as Mom's protector and provider. He was almost like the dad I grew up with—strong and yet loving. This is the first time I've caught a glimpse of this dad since before the accident. She shook her head as she searched for baking powder. For sure, his return to his old self was a welcome change. But what in the world had brought on his sudden compassion? She tried to think of any new influences in her father's life. The only thing she could come up with was Pastor Dave. Had his visits or the men's breakfast he'd attended influenced Dad in some way? For good? Maybe she owed the kind pastor a thank you the next time she saw him.

Dismissing the thought and refocusing on baking, she checked the coffee cake recipe in her mom's favorite cookbook. She probably could prepare the dish without having to go to the store for ingredients. She smiled, admitting to herself her mother was right. The coffee cake would smell wonderful baking while they decorated.

Decorations! The thought jarred her, as she realized the boxes of decorations were no doubt still in the attic. Obviously, Dad couldn't climb up there to get them. *Does that mean Mom's been getting the decorations down every year since the accident? Apparently so.* Lilly sighed. Mom couldn't do that now—no telling how she'd get sidetracked and what she'd end up bringing back down with her. *I'll have to go up and get the boxes since I'm the only one who is able.*

As she pulled down the ladder leading to the attic and climbed up, she thought of the many times she'd gone into what seemed in her childhood an almost magical room. Some of her best memories had taken place in the attic, as she and her mother dug through the various boxes and piles of memorabilia. Her mother almost always shared a story about every piece they came across.

I wonder if she could do that now. I learned at group how she might forget a lot of what's going on now, but she could retain much of her older memories. I suppose that's why she still thinks I'm in college. I guess there's no need to keep trying to convince her otherwise.

Lilly moved what looked like a promising box, releasing a swirl of dust into the air. As she held back a sneeze, she checked the labeling on the box. "Christmas decorations," she read aloud. "Wonderful!" She set the box down and looked at the other two boxes in the same area. Sure enough, they were Christmas decorations as well. After doing a quick spot check of the area and not finding any other Christmas-related boxes, she decided this was all there was. Now to drag them to the stairs and maneuver them down, one at a time. As she did so, she developed a new respect for her mom, as she thought again about her doing this chore—not to mention putting the decorations back after the holidays—since her father had been on his walker. What else had her mom had to do since the accident?

The thought kept her mind occupied, as she finally managed to get the boxes into the living room. Now to get the tree down from the roof of the car and into the house, where it would stand majestically in front of the picture window in the living room. Not until she'd wrestled the tree into the house did she realize she'd forgotten to look for the tree stand while she was up in the attic.

With a resigned sigh, she again pulled down the attic stairs and climbed upward to the room that had now lost the magical charm she felt as a child.

Rachel awoke with a start, frightened for a moment. She knew where she was, of course, and she recognized the daylight. But something seemed off.

She glanced to her right and was surprised to see Pete lying there, sound asleep. Rachel frowned. Why was he sleeping in his clothes? Was he sick?

She glanced down at her own clothes. She too was dressed, though she'd apparently thrown a blanket over herself. Dismissing the thought and gently touching Pete's forehead, she was relieved to find he didn't have a fever. She pushed back a thin strand of gray hair, one of the few remaining on his head. When had he gotten so bald? It seemed just yesterday he had started losing his hair, and now it was almost gone.

She shook her head. "You're getting old, my love," she whispered, her hand still touching his forehead.

Pete cracked open one eye. "You just now noticed?"

She pulled her hand away. "I didn't mean to wake you."

"You didn't. Actually, I didn't really sleep—just drifted in and out a little."

Rachel nodded. "I thought maybe you were sick, since you were sleeping in your clothes." She felt confused for a moment. "You weren't taking a nap, were you? You never take naps."

"I don't know about never. I do once in a while, though usually in my chair, while I'm watching TV."

His explanation didn't help explain why they were sleeping in their clothes, so she changed the subject. "I'm hungry," she announced. "How about some breakfast?"

Pete opened both eyes wide. "Breakfast? We had breakfast hours ago. Don't you remember? Lilly fixed it for us, and then she took us to—"

"Lilly's here?" Rachel threw off her cover, then sat up and scooted to the edge of the bed, where she quickly pushed her bare feet into her waiting slippers. "What's she doing home from school again? She's never going to graduate if she keeps missing classes."

Pete sighed as he got out of bed, but Rachel didn't wait for him. She was out of the bedroom and halfway down the hall when she smelled something wonderful.

"Lilly? Are you here?"

Lilly stepped into the living room doorway. "You're up," she said, smiling. "Did you have a good nap?"

Rachel felt even more confused. She couldn't remember if she'd had a nap or not. "Something smells awfully good."

Lilly smiled. "Oh. You're probably smelling the combination of the Christmas tree and a couple of scented candles I found in the attic. And I also found everything we need to make apple cider and a coffee cake. We can put the cake together, then sip cider and decorate the tree while it bakes."

Rachel frowned again. Why didn't Lilly's words make sense? What was she talking about? "What tree?"

This time Lilly was the one who drew her brows together. "The Christmas tree. The one you and Dad and I brought home a couple hours ago."

Slowly, Rachel began to shake her head. "No. No. No. We did not go get a tree together. I would have known if we'd done that. And besides, why would we? Is it Christmas already?" She pushed past Lilly and headed for the living room. If they had a tree, that's where she'd find it.

Sure enough, a lovely Douglas Fir stood upright in the red metal tree stand, its branches as yet unadorned. Admittedly, it was a beautiful tree; but why hadn't they included her when they picked it out? She scolded herself for being so childish, but her heart still hurt from the slight.

"Isn't it a perfect tree?" Lilly asked. "You were right. You saw the tree and said it was perfect for us. So are you ready to help make the cider and put the coffee cake into the oven? Then we can come back in here with Dad and decorate this tree."

Rachel turned, telling herself to be calm. Why would her daughter say she'd picked out the tree when she hadn't even been with them when they bought it?

Pete stood beside Lilly, his hands grasping his walker as he looked from mother to daughter and back, as if studying them both.

"Are you in on this too?" Rachel asked.

Pete scowled. "What are you talking about?"

"You know exactly what I'm talking about. You and Lilly. You went and got this tree without me, and now you're trying to make me believe I picked it out." She shook her head. "Why would you do that?"

Before Pete could answer, Lilly laid her hand on Rachel's shoulder. "Mom, it's okay, really. We don't have to talk about the tree right now. Let's go into the kitchen and get the cider. Then, if you feel up to it, we'll make the coffee cake."

Cider sounded good, and her legs felt weak; so she turned and headed for the kitchen. She'd scarcely had time to pull out a chair at the table before she sat, covered her face with her hands, and started to cry.

Pete didn't know what to think, and he certainly didn't know what to do. One minute Rachel talked to him as if everything were perfectly normal, and the next ... well, the next minute things were obviously not normal at all.

What bothered him most was wondering how to relate to this woman he'd been married to for decades yet scarcely knew. Guilt stabbed him as he remembered he'd been dependent on Rachel for nearly everything since the accident. Had he been at least partially responsible for her mind going off the rails?

He had retired to his favorite spot in the TV room, leaving Lilly to deal with her sobbing mother. *I should be in there with them. I should at least help. But how? What should I do or say?*

He had automatically flipped on the TV just before he sank down into his favorite chair, but he'd paid no attention to whatever program was on. The voice droned on in the background, as Pete continued to argue with himself. The guilt overwhelmed him—a guilt starting a long time ago—a guilt only now he was willing to admit.

On the other hand, even if he were partially to blame for Rachel's condition—and he wasn't at all sure he was— Lilly had shared enough with him to realize the disease couldn't be reversed and would, undoubtedly, get worse. This was a no-win situation for both of them.

And what about Lilly? This can't be fun for her, watching her mother deteriorate and not being able to prevent the progression. He sighed. *But at least she tries. She goes to those group meetings and talks to Pastor Dave occasionally. What do I do? Just sit here and feel sorry for myself?*

Pete realized he'd been growing increasingly bitter and resentful over the past few years, but never had he felt as low as he did at this moment.

His silent cry wrenched his heart, forcing tears from his eyes. *What am I going to do? How can I help?*

The answer came from deep inside: *If you let me, I will carry you.*

Pete swallowed a sob. Was God truly talking to him? The idea was a difficult concept for him to accept; but then again, who else could it be? And did he dare respond to the words he'd heard? He took a deep breath and decided to try.

"What should I do, God?" he whispered. "Show me, please!"

Call Pastor Dave, came the answer. *Call him now.*

Pete felt his eyes go wide. He could no longer deny the voice. Either he had become crazier than Rachel, or the very God of the universe was speaking to him.

He hoisted himself up on his walker and made his way to the phone in the bedroom. If he was going to call the pastor and talk about something as personal as his wife's sanity—not to mention his own—he wanted some privacy.

Chapter 24

Lilly heaved a sigh of relief. Her mom seemed to be settling down at last. She was no longer sobbing and had even managed to drink her cider. When Lilly suggested they make the coffee cake together, her mother had seemed excited.

"There. It's in the oven," Lilly said, smiling at Mom, a smudge of flour on her cheek. Lilly resisted her impulse to wipe the flour away and instead decided to see how much of the day her mom remembered. "Let's set the timer and then get started on the tree. What do you think?"

Her mother's brown eyes lit up. "We have a tree?"

Lilly nodded. "We do, Mom, just waiting for us to decorate." Lilly wanted to remind Mom she had picked it out but remembered what she'd learned in group—keep unnecessary information to a minimum.

Lilly set the timer, then led the way to the living room, calling out to her father to join them. She wasn't sure he would, but she wanted him to know he was welcome.

As they stepped into the room, Mom gasped and clapped her hands together. "It's perfect! This tree is absolutely perfect." She beamed as she turned to Lilly. "Did I pick it out?"

Lilly swallowed the lump in her throat. "You did, Mom. And you're right—it's perfect."

They began opening the boxes of Christmas decorations and hadn't gotten far when Dad pushed his walker into the room. "So tell me what you want me to do," he said. "I see you've already got the tree in the stand. You should have asked me. I would have helped."

"Thanks, Dad," Lilly said, her smile sincere. "I'm so glad you're going to help us."

They were down to one last box of decorations when the timer sounded from the kitchen. "Finally! My mouth has been watering since we put that thing in the oven. It smells scrumptious!"

"It sure does," Mom said, turning to Dad. "Lilly made the cake, but I helped."

Dad's eyes dimmed before he smiled at his wife. "That's great, sweetheart. With my two best girls working on it, I know it's going to be good."

In minutes, they were back in the kitchen, sipping more cider and tasting the cake, which had barely had time to cool. The smell of cinnamon permeated the air, as they talked and laughed about Christmases past.

Just like they told me in group. Mom seems to remember those previous Christmases better than the recent ones. Lilly sighed. *I guess I'd better appreciate her lucid moments now, as they'll no doubt diminish with time.*

She got up to get the coffee pot and refill their cups, but Dad begged off. "I had two cups with breakfast this morning, and two more when we were out for lunch. I think I've hit my limit—and then some."

"What about a second piece of coffee cake?" Lilly asked, looking from her father to her mother and back.

Dad shook his head. "Maybe later."

Mom appeared undecided but finally said, "No more. I'm full."

"Then let's get back to work on the tree," Lilly said.

Dad began to push himself up from the table and onto his walker; but her mother sat still, a puzzled look on her face.

"What's wrong, Mom?" Lilly asked. "Don't you want to finish decorating the tree?"

"What tree?"

Lilly exchanged glances with her father as he stood by his walker beside his wife's chair. Then he laid a hand on her shoulder, obviously at a loss for words.

"We got a Christmas tree this morning, Mom," Lilly said, keeping her voice calm and even. "Remember?"

Mom frowned. "I don't think so."

Hot tears bit the back of Lilly's eyes, and she wondered if she would be able to hold them back. What should she say now? She didn't want to cause her mom to have another meltdown.

Before Lilly could decide what to say, her mother's expression changed from confusion to delight. "Yes, let's go decorate the tree." She pushed her chair back with a loud scrape and nearly jumped to her feet. "Come on, Pete," she said, smiling up at him. "Let's decorate the tree together." She glanced back at Lilly. "The three of us."

Lilly's heart warmed. Maybe they'd survive the day after all.

Back in the living room, hanging decorations and then standing back to discuss whether or not they were in the right place, their conversation seemed as natural as it had this morning. And then they were ready to hang the last colored globe.

Mom cupped a final decoration in her hands as she let out a soft sob.

"What's wrong, Mom?" Lilly asked, as both she and Dad turned to look at her mother. "Are you all right? Did we forget something?"

Slowly, Mom shook her head. "What are we going to do now? This is the last decoration."

"But that's a good thing, right?" Dad asked with seemingly forced cheerfulness. Lilly met Dad's gaze and mouthed, "Thank you."

Mom continued to shake her head, as tears glistened in her brown eyes. When some spilled over onto her cheek, she sobbed. "This is the last decoration," she repeated. "What will we do then?" She glanced from her husband to her daughter, her voice cracking as she spoke. "How can we do the next thing if we don't know what the next thing is?"

Mom was once again stuck on *do the next thing*, and Dad wasn't going to be able to handle the situation. Lilly doubted if she could either, but she had to try.

She stepped next to her mom and put an arm around her waist. "Mom, don't you remember? After we hang this last decoration, we're going to turn off the house lights and turn on the tree lights. Then we're going to sit here on the couch together and sing Christmas carols."

Lilly wasn't sure where the idea had come from, but it seemed to be working. Mom's sobs faded, replaced by a hopeful sparkle in her eye. "Oh, I think that would be wonderful!" She held out the last decoration. "Hurry up and hang this last ornament, Pete. I want to see the tree lit up."

Dad raised his eyebrows, seemingly surprised at Mom's change in mood. "Sure, okay," he said at last. "You two sit down there on the sofa, and I'll take care of the lights."

Feeling a weight lift from her shoulders, Lilly escorted her mother to the sofa, where they sat down, side-by-side, leaving just enough room for her dad to join them.

✷❋✿❖

Saturday morning arrived far too quickly, at least as far as Pete was concerned. He was already second-guessing the call he'd made to Pastor Dave, asking if they could chat sometime. The pastor had offered to pick him up for the special Christmas men's breakfast so they could talk on the way to the restaurant. Pete had agreed, but now wondered what the pastor could possibly say to make things better with Rachel. He also marveled at how quickly the time had passed since he'd first attended the men's breakfast last week.

When the doorbell rang, Lilly got to the door before Pete. As he grabbed his jacket from the entryway closet, Lilly opened the door, no doubt wondering what the pastor was doing there.

"It's for me," he said, pushing his walker up behind Lilly. "We're … uh … going to breakfast."

Lilly turned, her brown eyes wide. Her short reddish-gold hair shone under the entryway light. For a brief moment, Pete thought what a beautiful woman his daughter had become. *Like her mother.*

"I didn't realize," Lilly said, then stepped back to let her father through.

Pete pushed the walker out the door, immediately wishing he'd taken the time to don his jacket, rather than just draping it over the walker bar in case he needed it later. Obviously, he needed his jacket now. Since he didn't want to hold things up any longer than necessary, he kept moving toward the dark blue Honda Civic parked in front of the house.

Pastor Dave hurried up beside him and opened the passenger door, then folded up the walker and put it in the trunk before climbing into the car himself.

"So," he said, as he looked back over his shoulder to check for traffic. After waiting for an old multi-colored pickup to sputter past them, Pastor Dave pulled out into the street. "How are things with Rachel? Any change since you called me?"

Pete was surprised the pastor had jumped right in, rather than allowing for a customary exchange of pleasantries before going for the jugular. Taking a deep breath, Pete recalled he was the one who had called to arrange this, not the pastor. He should respond accordingly.

"Not really," Pete said, keeping his eyes straight forward. "She still has some good days—well, good hours, really—but a lot more bad ones than even a couple months ago. Or, at least, it seems that way."

"Mm. Sounds about right. There's no set pattern or timeframe for how these things progress, I'm afraid. But you're wise to take advantage of those good times whenever possible. I promise you, they will be some of your sweetest memories when"—he took a deep breath— "when she passes."

Unwelcomed tears bit Pete's eyes. He pushed them back, determined not to fall apart in front of someone. So far, he'd been able to limit his meltdowns to when he was alone.

"I"—he swallowed before going on—"I want to help her, but I'm just not sure how to. Lilly seems to handle Rachel's bad moments so much better than I do."

The pastor chuckled. "Women do that," he said, his voice reassuring. "We men are terrible at it."

Pete turned his head toward Pastor Dave. "So, you're telling me I'm not the only one who puts his foot in his mouth almost daily."

The pastor shot a quick glance in Pete's direction before redirecting his attention to the road. "Not at all, my friend. I'm afraid that's just what we do."

For some reason, the pastor's words seemed to help.

"I think the worst part," Pete said, "is knowing she's not going to get better. I'm going to keep losing her, a little at ..." His voice cracked. "A little at a time. And then ..."

"And then she'll die," the pastor said, finishing Pete's thought.

Abrupt ... but true. Pete hung his head. "Yeah. Exactly."

Pastor Dave turned on the blinker and made a right turn. They were very near the restaurant now, and Pete was determined not to continue this personal conversation in the presence of the other men from church. Before he could finish his thought, Pastor Dave spoke. "Pete, I don't mean to push you; but I think it's important for us to talk about eternal matters. Knowing what will happen to Rachel when she dies will help you deal with the loss when the time comes."

A red flag began to wave in Pete's mind, and he felt his heart quicken. Why had he thought he should talk to the pastor about the situation with Rachel? Why hadn't he realized the conversation would end up on the heaven-and-hell topic?

He cleared his throat. "Um, yeah. I suppose."

The pastor pulled into the parking lot, stopping at the far end, away from most other cars. Pete's red flag was waving faster now.

Pastor Dave shut off the engine and turned to face Pete. *Now what?* Pete held his breath.

"Pete, it's not like you haven't heard the gospel. Before your accident, you came to church with Rachel off and on. And I know she's told you about the Lord."

Pete's throat was dry. All he could do was nod.

The pastor continued. "Knowing about the gospel or even being a good man is not enough. To truly know God is to make the gospel message personal. There's no other way, Pete. None."

Pete took a deep breath, determined to tell Pastor Dave he didn't want to talk about any of this after all. Before he could open his mouth to say a word, he felt a warmth washing over him, melting his heart and unleashing a torrent of tears.

Before he knew what was happening, Pete began to sob and pray, repeating the pastor's words as they clasped hands together. Though the words scarcely registered in his mind, Pete had asked God to forgive him—and he had—no doubt was now left in Pete's heart.

✳ ❋ ✧ ❖

Pete had never been happier. In fact, he couldn't remember a time when he'd even come close to being this happy. Bubbles of joy kept popping up from somewhere deep within, and he didn't know if he were going to break out in laughter or tears of joy. Surprisingly, though he was in a public place with people he scarcely knew, he wasn't concerned about letting his happiness show—no small change for a man used to masking his emotions at all costs.

They'd understand. He scanned around the half-dozen guys seated at the table with him. *They've all had this same experience at some point. No wonder they seem so happy and positive.*

"... a new brother in Christ," the pastor said, interrupting Pete's thoughts. "We're so glad you're here with us, Pete."

Pete had been so engrossed in his own emotions he hadn't realized the men at the table were smiling at him, offering words of welcome and love. Apparently, Pastor Dave had told them about Pete's experience out in the car before they came inside. Less than an hour earlier, he would have deeply resented someone sharing something so personal without his permission, but now he didn't mind. In fact, the others rejoicing with him only added to his happiness.

He blinked back tears and struggled to get past the lump in his throat. "Thanks," he said at last. "I finally know what it means to truly know God, to realize he loves me. Me!" He shook his head in amazement. "I can't help but wonder why."

The man on his left, who Pete remembered was named Jim, clapped him on the shoulder. "We understand completely," he said, then looked around at the group. "Don't we, guys?"

All of them agreed, speaking words of encouragement and camaraderie.

"We've all been there," Jim said. "I think of the wonder of salvation every day, even after all the years I've walked with the Lord. But I have to remind myself this salvation isn't about my goodness or worthiness—salvation is all about the goodness and worth of Jesus."

"Amen," Pastor Dave said. "From this day and forever, Pete, when God looks at you, he sees Jesus."

Pete could only nod and brush away a tear. He felt he had finally come home, and he couldn't wait to tell Rachel all about his conversion. He had asked Jesus to come into his life, and he now knew without a doubt Jesus was his Lord and Savior.

The waitress came up to the table and took their orders. Pete asked for coffee only—he was far too excited to eat.

"So, Pete," Jim asked, "are you and your family planning a big Christmas celebration?"

Pete set his cup down. He had no idea what, if anything, these new brothers of his knew about Rachel's situation, but he realized he could speak freely and safely with them about the situation.

"Actually," he said, "we'll probably keep the holidays low-key. My wife has"—he took a deep breath—"my wife has Alzheimer's, and it's progressing. Our grown daughter has come home to stay with us and to help out." He shook his head. "I'm not sure how we'd manage without her."

The man directly across from Pete cleared his throat. "We're sorry to hear this, Pete. That must be really tough."

Pete nodded. "It is. But right now, I feel like things are going to get better. Not my wife's illness, but the way we live and cope with her Alzheimer's." He glanced at Pastor Dave before asking, "Does that make sense?"

The pastor's dark eyes reflected his smile. "Absolutely. God hasn't promised to take away all our problems or difficulties, but he has promised to walk through them with us—to carry us when we're too weak to walk."

Pete turned back to the others. "That's exactly what I needed to hear. Thanks, all of you. It's so good to know you all care and understand, even if you've never been around anyone with Alzheimer's."

"I haven't," Jim said. "Not personally. But I know there's nothing too hard for God, and we're going to be praying for you and your family daily."

Scattered *amens* echoed around the table, just as the waitress came with their breakfast orders. After setting their plates in front of them, she refilled Pete's cup. "Are you sure I can't get you anything else?"

Pete smiled up at her. "No, thank you. I've got absolutely everything I need."

Chapter 25

Pete walked from the car to the house, feeling like a new man. Lilly met him in the entryway as he walked in the front door. "Welcome back." She smiled. "You look like you had a good time."

"I did," he said. "Where's your mother? I need to tell her something."

"She's lying down for a while. She should be up soon. Can it wait?"

"Sure. The news will be just as good in an hour as it is now."

Lilly raised her eyebrows. "News? I'd love to hear your news. How about telling me over a cup of coffee? I can make a fresh pot."

Pete waved away the offer. "No more coffee," he said. "I think I drank a gallon at the restaurant. But yes, I'd be happy to tell you my news."

They made their way into the kitchen and sat down across from one another at the table. "So ..." Lilly said. "Your news?"

Pete smiled, already feeling the bite of tears at the back of his eyelids, not tears of sadness, rather tears of joy. "I hope I can get through this without crying. I'll try."

Lilly's face appeared more than slightly surprised. "I've never known that to be a problem for you before."

Pete chuckled. "I'm sure that's true. But then, I've never had the experience I did today."

Lilly leaned forward a bit, obviously anxious to hear what he had to say.

"I ..." He paused. How could he express what happened to him this morning? Even if he could verbalize the experience, would she understand? He took a deep breath. "I received Jesus as my Savior today. I prayed with Pastor Dave and asked God to forgive me." His voice broke, and he paused to collect himself. "And he did. He forgave me for so very much."

The tears were back, and he grabbed a napkin from the holder at the center of the table to wipe them away. He focused on Lilly's face. Why didn't she say something? Had she heard what he said?

Slowly, she shook her head, her eyes wide. "I can't believe what I'm hearing. Are you serious?"

"More serious than I've ever been about anything in my life." He grinned. "And happier than I've ever been too."

Their eyes locked for a moment, as he watched various emotions play out on her face. Before she could speak, Rachel came into the room.

"Well, here you are. Is it time for breakfast?" She looked around the kitchen. "No coffee?"

Lilly pulled her eyes away from her father and looked up at Rachel. "I'll make some right now," she said. "And then I'll leave you two to talk."

Rachel was confused. Why had Lilly put the coffee on and then left? The aroma of coffee brewing permeated the room, and she sat next to her husband, wondering if she should ask him to fix breakfast or wait until Lilly returned. *Or maybe it's time for lunch. Maybe I should fix lunch. I'm sure I know how to, don't I?*

"Are you hungry, Pete?" Why did he look so happy? She couldn't remember seeing him smile much at all for a very long time. But then, she forgot things, so this might be one of those things she'd forgotten.

Pete shook his head. "No, sweetheart. I'm not hungry. I went to breakfast with the men from church. Pastor Dave took me."

Rachel gasped. Was this something else she'd forgotten? Had Pete started going to church? What was going on?

He patted her hand. "Everything's all right," he said, his voice reassuring. "In fact, I have some really wonderful news for you."

"You do?"

He smiled. "I finally understand what you meant when you told me about your relationship with Jesus. You said it was about more than just going to church and being a good person. You told me your faith was based on knowing God personally and having Jesus as your Savior." He squeezed her hand and leaned toward her. "I understand now because I asked God to forgive me, and I received Jesus as *my* Savior."

Rachel's cheeks heated, and she suspected they were turning crimson. For just a moment, she had difficulty breathing. Was this some sort of joke? Was she just imagining Pete's words? She'd known for some time her memory wasn't what it should be and was getting worse. But this ...

She shook her head, as if to clear out the confusion. "What are you saying, Pete? What are you telling me?"

Pete lifted her hand to his lips and gently kissed it. "I'm telling you I'm now a Christian, a believer ... like you."

Tears stung her eyes as she tried to absorb her husband's words. If what he said was true, this was an answer to her most heartfelt prayer, something she'd talked to God about for years.

She swallowed. "I don't know what to say."

Pete grinned. "How about 'welcome to the family'?"

Rachel nodded, nearly unable to speak. She couldn't wait to call Lilly and tell her the news, though she'd have to wait until later in the day, when her daughter was no longer in class. Would Lilly appreciate what had happened with her father? She hadn't attended church regularly for quite some time, although she accepted Jesus as her Savior at a summer Bible camp years earlier.

No matter. All Rachel knew was that she had to tell Lilly the news. And then, after she'd told Lilly, she'd call Pastor Dave and tell him.

Wait a minute. Hadn't Pete said he was with the pastor earlier? Did Pastor Dave already know what had happened?

So many questions swirling around in her mind. Rachel wanted to ask Pete or Pastor Dave about everything, but she was beginning to feel overwhelmed. Tears wet her cheeks, and Pete always got upset when she cried. She swiped at her tears, willing them away, to no avail.

"I'm sorry," she sobbed, covering her face with her hands. "I'm trying not to cry, but ..."

The next thing she knew, her husband was pulling her chair closer to his and taking her in his arms. "It's all right, sweetheart," he crooned, stroking her hair as he held her. "If you need to cry, you just go ahead. I've been doing some of that myself today."

Rachel couldn't believe her ears. She could scarcely remember when Pete used to talk to her or treat her so gently and lovingly. Did she dare believe what he had said—about knowing Jesus? She wanted to believe this, but so much of what she thought she knew these days turned out not to be true.

"I don't know much about how to pray yet, God," she heard Pete say, "but please help my beautiful wife understand what I'm telling her, to know we now share the same faith in you. Help her, Father, please."

In the midst of all the uncertainty, in spite of all the questions and fears demanding her attention, she heard a familiar voice speak her name: *Rachel. I am here with you. Always. And with Pete.*

Her fears melted as she rested in the arms of both her husband and her Father—the first time she could remember feeling such peace in a very long time.

The next morning, Lilly and her father had another chance to talk alone. Lilly was making breakfast, and her mother was getting ready for church.

"Mom sure seemed excited yesterday." Lilly focused on his father's expressions ... similar yet different. "Was it because of what you told Mom ... about your relationship with Jesus? She didn't say much, but I assumed as much."

Her father sat at the table, sipping his coffee. "It was. I think she was a bit overwhelmed by what I said, but she was definitely happy."

Lilly continued stirring the oatmeal. "So your talk went well, then."

"It did," he said, setting his cup down on the table and fixing his glance on it while he spoke. "As I said, I think she was overwhelmed ... but in a good way." He looked up. "Do you know what I mean?"

"I think I do. And I knew she'd be happy about what happened."

"And how about you?" he asked. "Now that you've had a little time to think about it, how do you feel?"

Lilly lifted her eyebrows in surprise. "What do you mean, how do I feel? I told you yesterday—I think it's great."

"For me," he said. "You think it's great for me. And for your mom too. But what about for you? You used to go to church, and I remember you telling me how much Jesus loved me and how I should be a Christian. Do you remember?"

Lilly stared at the bubbling oatmeal, a slight ringing in her ears. "That was a long time ago, Dad. I was just a kid."

"Maybe." He took another drink of coffee. "But was the experience real? Did you know God then? Looking back from my current perspective, I think you had found something special."

"I believed in God, if that's what you mean," Lilly said, annoyed her resentment tainted her words. "And I still do, though I've had doubts off and on. Basically, I do believe God exists."

Dad smiled, with more understanding than she'd seen in a long time. "You know I'm not just talking about believing in God. Most of the time, I believed in him too—believed he existed. But until yesterday, I never knew him personally." He shook his head. "And now I do. I met him, Lilly, and found out he loved me. Talk about amazing!" He paused before going on. "So I'm asking you … did you know him in a personal way when you were younger? Did you really know he loved you and forgave you? And if you did, what changed?"

Lilly nearly slammed the spoon on the counter beside the stove. She jerked her head up and glared at her father. "I grew up," she declared. "That's what happened. And then I married Jacob. His family is Jewish—as you know. He didn't really practice his faith, and I suppose I didn't either. But we both believed in God … sort of … and I still do … now. Period. End of discussion, okay?"

Her father sat slack-jawed, as if stunned at the intensity of his daughter's reaction. "I remember Pastor Dave warning me not everyone would react favorably to my conversion," Dad said, his voice cracking with emotion, "but I never imagined I'd evoke such a negative response from my own daughter."

Chapter 26

Did her face radiate her joy? This was happiness, sitting in church, with Lilly on one side and Pete on the other—the thing Rachel had prayed for and dreamed of for years. Here she sat between the two people she loved the most. Every song they sang during worship, Rachel felt as if her heart would burst and she'd fly right off to heaven. She smiled, remembering her favorite song, "I'll Fly Away."

Despite her joy, she was slightly disappointed Lilly didn't join in the worship. She was nearly certain her daughter had at least participated in the singing when she'd joined Rachel at church the past few weeks. *Then again, most of the time I can't trust my memory.*

Pete, on the other hand, seemed to be doing his best to follow along, reading the words from the overhead screen. And throughout Pastor Dave's sermon, he appeared to be taking in every word.

You're so good to me, Father. You've answered my prayers and brought Pete into relationship with you. Now I know we'll be together for all eternity.

God's response was immediate. *That is very true, daughter. And Lilly will be there too.*

The promise brought tears to Rachel's eyes, as she ventured a quick peek at her daughter, who stared straight ahead. *She's a good girl, Lord. But I do hope she'll stop missing so much school just to stay home and take care of me. She needs to graduate, Father. What will become of her if she doesn't?*

Again, the answer was immediate. *I will take care of her.*

Rachel's shoulders relaxed as she realized her beloved daughter was in God's hands. No matter how many things she'd forget or how confused or frightened she'd become, she was confident she could trust the Lord with her daughter's future as well as her own. *I always want to be able to hear your voice, Father. As long as I know you're near, I can handle all the rest.*

And so it shall be, he whispered. *Always.*

When Sunday evening came, Lilly finished her latest writing assignment, attached it to an email, and sent it zipping through cyberspace to her editor. Now to break the news to her parents she had an offer on her home and had to leave right after Christmas to get things settled. She wouldn't be gone long, but she worried about leaving them alone.

She considered trying to explain the reasons to her mother, but decided to let Dad manage while she would be gone. Admittedly, he'd been making a lot more effort to help out lately. He'd even told her he was considering going to the support group with her, though they'd have to find someone to stay with Mom while they were gone. *Pastor Dave is always saying to call if we need anything. I just might take him up on his offer.*

Even more amazing, Dad had told her he was also considering going to physical therapy. "I know I should have gone ages ago," he'd said, "and it may be too late to get much benefit out of it. But I should at least try. Right?"

Lilly shut down her computer and headed toward the kitchen for a final cup of tea before turning in for the night. She'd just put the kettle on when Dad came rattling in on his walker, wearing his pajamas and a robe.

"Hey, Dad," she said. "Can't sleep? I'm about to have a cup of tea. Want to join me?"

He shrugged. "You know I'm not much of a tea man, but why not? I sure don't need any coffee at this hour."

Lilly grabbed another mug and soon had two steaming cups on the table in front of them, as they sat across from one another. "So you didn't answer my question," she said.

Dad raised his eyebrows. "Sorry. What question?"

"I asked if you were having trouble sleeping."

"Ah. Yes. I guess I am"—he grinned—"but in a good way. I went to bed, thinking I was tired and would drop right off. Your mother beat me to slumberland—out like the proverbial light the minute her head hit the pillow. But me? All I could do was think about how blessed I am to know God. And that He loves me ..." He shook his head. "I keep thinking it's too good to be true, but then I remember it *is* true. All of it. Every word in the Bible. Every promise in his Word. I guess I just can't sleep because I'm too full of wonder and amazement."

Lilly squirmed in her seat, trying to escape the feeling, even while her heart whispered, "Stay." She truly was happy for Dad and for what his conversion meant for Mom. *Where does this leave me? Am I ready to recommit my life to God?* Childhood memories had called to her for years, but the voice had grown stronger and more persistent lately.

She realized her father was watching her, waiting for her to respond. She smiled. "That's wonderful, Dad. It really is. I'm very happy for you."

He reached across the table and patted her hand. "Thank you, sweetheart. And thank you for all you're doing for us. Don't think for a minute I don't appreciate it. I know you've given up a lot to be here."

"Don't worry, Dad. I'm just glad I'm in a position to be able to be here. I do miss teaching, but I can always go back to that later. And I'm still getting my writing assignments done and turned in. A good thing. Right? Oh, and I almost forgot to tell you. I have a buyer for the house. A young couple with two kids. The home will be perfect for them. I'm just surprised the house sold so quickly. We—Jacob and I—just listed it not long ago." The reminder she had hoped to raise children of her own in that house twisted her heart for a moment, but she pushed the thought aside. "I have to go back this week, right after Christmas, and get things settled. I'll be gone for three or four days. Will this be a problem for you and Mom?"

"Not at all. We'll be fine. If we need something, I'll call Pastor Dave. He's already asked me to call if I need anything, so I know he won't mind."

Lilly nodded. "That's good. I thought of trying to explain why I'm leaving to Mom, but I'm not sure she'd understand or remember."

He shook his head. "No need. And you're right. She probably wouldn't understand. She'll just think you've returned to school, and she'll be happier when you get back."

Lilly smiled. "I'm so glad you and Mom are close again. You need to lean on each other."

"You're absolutely right. And since now we share the same faith, we'll be even closer than when we were young."

Doubt panged her soul. "Dad, you have to remember Mom's memory is worsening all the time. Even though you share her faith in God, she's not always going to remember you converted."

Her father patted her hand again. "I know. But that's okay." He smiled. "After all, your mother and I are going to spend eternity together. And her mind will be perfect then. Mine too. It doesn't get any better than that, right?"

Lilly swallowed the lump in her throat and blinked back hot tears. "Right," she said, her voice cracking. She got up to clear the table and head for bed.

Since her parents would be going together, Lilly had considered staying home from church on Christmas Eve. But she would have had to drive them there and pick them up, even if she didn't go inside. Might as well join them.

In addition to a bulletin, they were each handed a small candle for the end of the service. As they found an empty spot large enough for the three of them, about midway toward the front, Lilly decided she was glad she'd come. The church was beautifully decorated, and the scent of pine filled the air. And then, of course, there were all the children, bright-eyed and exuding excitement and energy.

It doesn't seem that long ago when I was that age. Her thoughts were filled with childhood memories as she settled into the seat nearest the aisle, her parents on either side, both looking nearly as excited as the children.

How did I let myself lose that sense of excitement? She thought back over the years and decided going to church lost excitement soon after she became a teenager. She had wanted to be cool, to be accepted by the so-called in crowd. Had she succeeded? She supposed she had, since she ended up being a cheerleader and a member of the Student Council. As she transitioned from her Christian friends to her popular ones, she had also transitioned from enjoying the presence of God to hanging out almost exclusively with those whose sole purpose was looking good and enjoying the good things life had to offer.

Thankfully, I never got into drinking or drugs. I don't know if it was my childhood faith holding me back or... Whatever prevented me from going too far, I'm grateful. Too many of the kids I knew then did, and who knows what's happened to them since?

Familiar Christmas carols played softly in the background, as people continued to fill the sanctuary.

Lilly was aware of them, but her mind was on her past. *Even when I was in college, I dropped into chapel now and then. And I did have a couple of Christian friends on campus. But then I met Jacob—or should I say, Mom introduced me to Jacob. I know she never dreamed anything would come of that introduction, and she was nearly devastated when we did fall in love. She tried to talk me out of the relationship, to make me understand the difficulties of being married to an unbeliever. I wouldn't listen.* Lilly sighed. *When Mom realized she couldn't change my mind, she did her best to support us and accept our news. But I can't help but wonder how many times she regretted introducing Jacob to me— even while she was doing everything she could to make sure I had the most beautiful wedding possible.*

Lilly reflected on the weekend she met Jacob. She'd been home for a visit, and Jacob dropped by to ask Mom about something at work. Sparks flew from the moment the two were introduced. No doubt her mother never gave the introduction a second thought, but Lilly hadn't been able to stop thinking about the slightly older man with the dreamy green eyes. When he finally managed to track down her number at college and call her, Lilly had been thrilled. For the most part, they'd been inseparable from that moment on—until, of course, they came to an impasse about having children. Lilly mentioned the adoption possibility if they couldn't have a child of their own, but her husband nixed the idea. Jacob was perfectly content with their lives as they were—both of them working and bringing in nice salaries and living in a lovely home in a great neighborhood. Lilly was not, though she tried to pretend she was. She didn't want to alienate her husband.

And how did that work out for you? The thought dripped with sarcasm. *Jacob moved on with his life, and I'm here taking care of my parents.* She sighed. *And the day after tomorrow, I have to leave to deal with all the details involved in selling the home Jacob and I bought together.*

Tears threatened, but as she so often did, she refused to let them take hold. *Everything worked out for the best. Jacob and I are just too different. We could never have come to a compromise on such a huge subject as whether or not to have children.*

Music caught her attention then, and she looked up to discover the worship team, standing on the podium, starting their first song. As the rest of the congregation rose to their feet, she joined them.

She'd nearly forgotten how much she loved the old carols she'd sung as a child. Funny how the words came right back to her, and she soon found herself singing along. By the time Pastor Dave took over the microphone and the congregation was seated once again, she found herself focused on his every word.

I've heard the story my whole life, but suddenly I can imagine God himself coming to earth as a helpless baby.

Tears fell, and she couldn't hold them back. When her mother handed her a tissue, she took it gratefully. She welcomed the semi-darkness when the lights were dimmed and the ushers proceeded down the aisles, lighting the candle of each person on the aisle seat near the center. Those with lighted candles were then instructed to light the candle of the person next to them, who would light the next person's candle, and so on. Lilly was pleased to see her mother handle the task without much confusion.

As the service came to a close, they were once again on their feet to sing the final song. At this moment, Lilly sensed the need to come home—back to the God she'd pledged to follow so many years earlier. *Forgive me, Father. Forgive me for staying away so long, and thank you for letting me come back to you. Help me to stay faithful, Lord. I don't want to stray again.*

The silent voice responded with warmth and acceptance. *Welcome home, dear child. I will hold you close to my heart.*

As the congregation exited the pews and moved down the aisle toward the doors, Lilly managed to stem her flow of tears. She knew they hovered nearby, waiting for an excuse to burst forth. *I won't be able to drive if I can't stop crying, Lord. Help me get us all home safely, please!*

Minutes later, as they pulled into the garage, she thanked God for answering her prayer. Now to share her news with her parents.

Epilogue

The night was cold and clear, the moon shining like a beacon toward the earth, bidding all to come to the One whose birth they would celebrate the next morning. Rachel tugged her coat tighter, trying to keep out the cold but not quite ready to go back inside. There was just too much for her to digest. First Pete, and now ...

She smiled as she stood in their familiar backyard, looking up to the heavens. "Thank you, Father," she whispered. "Thank you for letting me live long enough to see the answers to my prayers for my husband and child."

She heard the sliding glass door open and shut behind her, and then Pete joined her.

"It's awfully cold out here," he said as he slipped an arm around her shoulders. "Are you okay? We can go inside and have something hot to drink."

"Maybe later," she said. "I'm fine for now. Besides, you know how rare these clear nights are." She sighed. "I'm just trying to understand Lilly's news." She tilted her head and looked up at her husband. "She's back with the Lord now, isn't she?"

Even in the darkness, Rachel could see Pete's eyes shining. "She is," he said, squeezing her shoulders with his one-armed embrace. "We all are."

Rachel looked again at the night sky. "But she has to go back to school, doesn't she?"

Pete hesitated before answering. "She'll only be gone a few days, sweetheart. Then she'll be back here with us."

"I shouldn't be so selfish," she said. "I mean, I know she has to get back to school so she can graduate, but ..." She breathed deeply, her breath like mist in the night air.

"What is it, sweetheart?"

"It's just that ..." The words escaped her. Everything seemed to confuse or frighten her these days, whether logical or not. Lilly's leaving was no exception.

Help me, Lord. She swallowed and continued her prayer aloud. "It's just I'm not sure what we'll do while she's gone." Once again, she turned her head and looked up at her husband, no longer fighting the tears trickling down her cheeks. "Who will take care of me while she's gone?"

Pete's gaze was as tender as she'd ever seen, warming her heart, even as she shivered in the night air. He smiled. "Lilly taught me a new term," he said. "One she learned at her support group." He reached out and touched her cheek. "I will be your caregiver while she's gone, but I will also be your care-partner. That's the term she learned, and it describes us perfectly. We're partners, Rachel. Care-partners. You and me, whether Lilly's here to help or not. And besides, we have the greatest caregiver of all watching over us and loving us all the time."

How she loved hearing those words from her husband's lips, melting the fear always hovering so near. Then she asked him the question in her heart: "Do you love me, Pete?"

Her husband seemed surprised at first. But after a brief moment, he turned and pointed up at the sky. "You see the moon?"

She turned to look at the pale-yellow orb. "Yes," she said. "It's beautiful."

Pete pulled her from his side to stand in front of him, then drew her as close to his chest as he could, the walker between them. "I know it's not a harvest moon like that night so long ago." He kissed the top of her head. "The words I spoke were as true then as they are now. I will always love you—to the moon and back. Do you remember, sweetheart?"

Her tears wet the front of his jacket as she nodded and whispered, "Yes, I do. I do remember, my love. And I know I will never forget."

Making It Personal

(To be answered on your own and/or discussed in a group)

1. What is your personal experience, if any, with Alzheimer's?

2. What preconceived ideas and/or actual knowledge about Alzheimer's did you have before beginning this book?

3. How much of the book did you have to read before you realized Rachel had (or most likely had) Alzheimer's?

4. What were your initial emotions as you began to enter Rachel's world?

5. Were you able to relate to Pete or Lilly? If so, in what ways?

6. What surprises did you find in the book, whether specifically regarding Rachel, Pete, Lilly, or simply Alzheimer's in general?

7. Have you ever wondered if a loved one (or possibly even yourself) is displaying early signs of dementia/Alzheimer's? Did reading this book help confirm or deny your suspicions?

8. On a scale of 1-10, with 1 being slightly forgetful and 10 being a complete break with reality, where would you place the loved one who has shown signs of Alzheimer's?

9. As you read about Rachel's situation, why do you suppose she got stuck on her daughter being away

at college, when in reality, she'd been out of college for several years?

10. How did you feel about the fact, even though Rachel didn't understand and/or forgot quite a bit, she seemed to understand and remember when God spoke to her? How do you suppose her personal relationship with the Lord affected her progressing Alzheimer's? How might such a relationship help those you know who are fighting this otherwise heartbreaking disease?

Resources

❖ Alzheimer's Association (www.alz.org): 24/7 helpline: 1-800-272-3900; email-newsletters available (sign up online)

❖ ASPE (Office of the Assistant Secretary for Planning and Evaluation) Alzheimer's / Dementia | ASPE (hhs. gov)

❖ National Alzheimer's Project Act

❖ U.S. Department of Health and Human Services Alzheimer's Website

❖ National Institute of Aging Alzheimer's Disease Education and Referral Center

❖ National Alzheimer's Project Act Legislation

❖ National Plan to Address Alzheimer's Disease

❖ The International Alzheimer's Disease Research Portfolio (IADRP)

❖ AoA's Alzheimer's Disease Supportive Services Program (ADSSP)

❖ Priority Setting for Healthcare Performance Measurement--Alzheimer's Disease (2014)

❖ Cognitive Aging: Progress in Understanding and Opportunities for Action (2015)

❖ <u>2013-2014 Alzheimer's Disease Progress Report</u> <u>(2015)</u>

❖ <u>Disability and Care Needs of Older Americans: An</u> <u>Analysis of the 2011 National Health and Aging Trends</u> <u>Study (2014)</u>

About the Author

Kathi Macias (www.kathimacias.com) is the award-winning author of more than fifty books, including the 2011 Golden Scrolls Novel of the Year and 2011 Carol Award Finalist for *Red Ink*. A popular conference and retreat speaker, as well as wife, mother, grandmother, and great-grandmother, Kathi lives in Southern California with her husband, Al.

www.ingramcontent.com/pod-product-compliance
Lightning Source LLC
Chambersburg PA
CBHW051129020726
47501CB00005B/1419